D0699050

MID
—
AIR

Victoria Shorr

MID
—
AIR

Two Novellas

W. W. NORTON & COMPANY
Independent Publishers Since 1923

"Love Has No Pride" by Libby Titus and Eric Kaz © 1970 Libet Music (ASCAP) admin. by Wixen Music Publishing, Inc. All Rights Reserved. Used by Permission.

For information about permission to reproduce selections from this book, write to Permissions, W. W. Norton & Company, Inc., 500 Fifth Avenue, New York, NY 10110

For information about special discounts for bulk purchases, please contact W. W. Norton Special Sales at specialsales@wwnorton.com or 800-233-4830

Manufacturing by Lake Book Manufacturing
Book design by Brooke Koven
Production manager: Anna Oler

Library of Congress Cataloging-in-Publication Data

Names: Shorr, Victoria, author.
Title: Mid-air : two novellas / Victoria Shorr.
Description: First edition. | New York : W. W. Norton & Company, [2022]
Identifiers: LCCN 2021061123 | ISBN 9780393882100 (hardcover) | ISBN 9780393882117 (epub)
Subjects: LCGFT: Novellas.
Classification: LCC PS3619.H667 M53 2022 | DDC 813/.6—dc23/eng/20211217
LC record available at https://lccn.loc.gov/2021061123

W. W. Norton & Company, Inc.
500 Fifth Avenue, New York, N.Y. 10110
www.wwnorton.com

W. W. Norton & Company Ltd.
15 Carlisle Street, London W1D 3BS

1 2 3 4 5 6 7 8 9 0

To Sid, Fofie, and Ike,
Who walk in both worlds

They were making their fortune, just as we were losing ours.
We must have passed at one point in mid-air,
them on the way up, us free-falling.

—FROM AN UNPUBLISHED MANUSCRIPT

Great Uncle Edward

I

At eight o'clock the bell rang.

We were not, this time, sawing boards for table leaves, nor were we in the shower. We had said "dinner at eight," and knew this time that that meant that Great Uncle Edward, despite living on East Seventy-Second Street, really the hardest place from which to reach the West Village, would arrive at neither 7:55 nor 8:15. He would be there at eight, somehow, and he was.

Did he bring Cousin Betty in his taxi? This I can't remember, though I hope so. If not, rather than spend the few dollars herself, she would have paid her thirty-five cents and changed subways at Grand Central, taken the shuttle across. Always an unpleasant exercise, and in those days sometimes downright dangerous, especially for a frail woman already calling herself "elderly"—though, doing the terrible math of life, I realize she was not much older than I am now.

But then I was twenty-seven, and we had just moved to what seemed to me to be an entirely too upscale apartment on West Fourth Street from a much hipper loft in Little

Italy. A vast yawning place that loft had been, five flights up with windows all around and enough room for an archery course and dance floor. We couldn't stop the roof from leaking, so we put up a tent for a bedroom, lovely white canvas that the sun came through, and the truth is I've never liked any place better.

And there were the floors, through which anything that we dropped—crumbs, ashes, family rings—just sort of disappeared. Which was great for us, seeking freedom and "authenticity," as Hillary then Rodham had put it in a college speech a few years earlier; but not at all the thing for Uncle Edward. When we told him where we were living, he'd taken a sip of his bourbon and allowed that he'd walked through Little Italy "once, and caught the scarlet fever."

That would have been around 1906, when Uncle Edward was a young man.

Because by the time he came to dinner that night in the Village, he was old, older than anyone we'd ever known. In his nineties, back in 1978, when people didn't live that long. And indeed, everyone else in his generation of the family was long dead—his wife, his brothers and sisters, his cousins—but he was still waking up every morning and putting on his three-piece suit.

Just as he must have since—well, he wouldn't have worn a suit at St. Paul's School, or at Harvard, where he was class of "Aught Five," as they used to say. But maybe in the law school, and surely once that was finished, once he started work in New York at one of the firms down here. So add a few years, and you could conclude that Uncle Edward had been wearing some version of this suit for at least sixty-eight years.

Which was just as well now, for the warmth, since he was terribly thin, though still straight and tall and quite unbending, as we discovered the time we tried to go to the Westbury for dinner. It had seemed a good enough idea, since it was close to his apartment, but we hadn't reckoned on the revolving door, and I can still see Uncle Edward stuck inside one of the compartments, not quite fallen but listing heroically, like the mast of one of the clipper ships from which the family fortune had come. A hundred and fifty years ago, though, too long ago to do anyone who was left any more good.

At least in terms of money. But they all still knew who they were, so to speak, hence the three-piece suit, which was probably not out of place among the other ancients who still tottered up to the Century every day for lunch, as did Uncle Edward.

His only contemporary left there, though still five years his junior, was Judge Medina, famous for saving the country from the Communists in the Smith case in the late forties. But Judge Medina, though ninety, was still serving on the bench, which occasionally took him from the club at lunchtime, so then Uncle Edward would have to have his lunch with the writer he called "Zed" Mehta, who, though blind, could apparently manage his knife and fork well enough at the Century for Uncle Edward.

"Yes, Zed and I—" Uncle Edward would begin.

"*Ved*, Uncle Edward," Cousin Betty would occasionally suggest.

"As I said, Betty . . ." Uncle Edward would continue.

"Frightful to the girls at the *New Yorker*, I hear," Cousin Russell once put in. "They call them Vedettes."

I had in fact heard of them—girls like me, out of Wellesley or Radcliffe, whose way into the *New Yorker* was still through the typing test, and one of the stations along that way might be Ved Mehta's office. It seemed like the best of luck at first—a job at the *New Yorker*! And under the wing of a famous writer, no less.

But the demands of this particular job included not only eight hours per diem of longhand transcription of the blind author's memoirs, but also the daily confrontation with his hyped-up sense of smell, which in his case seemed not only to have replaced eyesight but to have brought a sort of license.

The girl would walk in, and Mehta would sniff, then ask if she had a new boyfriend. He claimed he could smell his aftershave, as well as other effluents, and it went from there, all day, with only fifteen minutes out for lunch, unless he was going across the street to the Century, where Uncle Edward would avenge them all by calling him "Zed."

Wholly unawares, but that was the point. "Ved," "Zed"— what was that to Uncle Edward?

And what might have brought the two of them together at the Century is rather a mystery—maybe Uncle Edward had inherited the esteemed writer from his brother, the editor. Maybe Mehta was too polite to change tables when his friend the editor died. Maybe Uncle Edward, well past the stage of bodily juices and aftershave, simply smelled right to Mehta. Or maybe men's clubs in that time and place didn't work that way at all. Maybe one sat with whom one sat.

Nor do we know whether to picture tall, thin, tottery, three-piece-suited Uncle Edward sitting in one of those chairs by a fire with his paper before or after lunch, as the details of his arrivals and departures at the club, though doubtless fixed, never made their way into our conversation. And though we'd like to know now, we didn't think to ask about it then, and now there's no one left to tell us if Uncle Edward took his taxi back uptown from Forty-Third Street right after lunch at two, or hung around there until four.

By which time it would have been getting on toward supper, which was a bit of a problem. Because though breakfast was a boiled egg and an English muffin, fixed by the woman who came in the mornings and "did for him," and lunch was settled at the club, supper still had to be solved every night, which was where we came into the picture.

I don't remember who first suggested it, who first mentioned that Great Uncle Edward, the last one remaining, and the eldest at that, was still alive and well and living in New York. Nor do I remember where we first met, though I do remember, exactly, what I wore. Because it was terribly important to me, being newly married and smitten with certain ideas, that Uncle Edward like me.

So I put on my new silk blouse, cream-colored, soft, drapey, bought on a lovely charge card with violets from Bonwit Teller's, one of the very first silks to come in to New York from Shanghai. Before, it had been all *Little Red Books* and those black canvas shoes, both of which I'd also bought but in Chinatown. This was something else. Not so much Chairman Mao as Last Emperor.

And I had a white duck skirt that I figured was probably the length that girls wore when Uncle Edward was dating, not that people dated in those days, or maybe they did? I do know that his two brothers married cousins whom they'd met at each other's wedding—I don't remember who married first and thus produced the cousin for the other one, though it's there in the books. But it must not have been easy, outside of weddings, to meet people you really liked in those days, so maybe they did date.

Or "call" or have ice cream on Sundays or whatever it was, but I thought that my clothes would look familiar to Uncle Edward, and they must have, because I felt that I'd passed muster, and that that was that. From then on, I probably could have shown up in little black shoes with the *Little Red Book*, and it wouldn't have fazed Uncle Edward. He still would have seen me in that floating white.

We might have met first at his apartment on East Seventy-Second, or simply joined up outside of Giovanni's, on East Fifty-Fifth. Uncle Edward was exactly what I had hoped he would be, I seemed to be some version of what he might have hoped had he thought about it, which he was probably too polite to do. His great-nephew, my husband, was blond and tall, in a pale green summer suit with one of his raw silk ties, also fitting the bill. Betty, his niece and the key to the whole evening, the one who must have made the introduction in the first place, would have rushed home from T. Y. Crowell on Fifty-Third, where she worked long days for low pay as a copy editor, taken a quick bath, combed her thinning gray-blond hair into a polite version, and put on one of her light blue dresses. She lived on First Avenue in the Fifties, and so could have walked to Giovanni's, which at least would have saved the thirty-five cents.

Wherever it was that we met up that night, I do know that we walked in together because I distinctly remember— who could forget?—old Mr. Giovanni, himself also a relic at that point, tottering up to us, and saying in his raspy old voice, "Same table, Mr. Perkins?" although Uncle Edward hadn't been there since his wife had died, in the forties.

The two men did not embrace, but they did their equivalent. Uncle Edward countered old Mr. Giovanni's "Same table?" with his own simple, "Thank you," nor did he slip into any show of emotion when his old friend, for what else could you call him at this point in life, came to the wonderful corner booth where we'd been seated to take our order himself.

"Lamb chops, Mr. Perkins?"

He'd remembered! For more than thirty years—Giovanni's! Is there any place like it anywhere anymore? One of those quiet, almost hushed, beautiful East Side establishments that was light—that is, pale—inside, not dark. Pale blue, as I recall, though I could be wrong, since it never occurred to us to take any pictures, because when you're twenty-seven, everything is still infinite. One will always be young and thrilled with life, and Giovanni's will always be there.

Pale blue, or perhaps beige, or grays, with those waiters—almost as old as the two ancient protagonists themselves, but tough guys still, every one of them. They looked like prototypes for the *Godfather* movies, only elderly versions, if any of those guys—Luca Brasi, Tessio—were to sidestep their sleep with the fishes and attain old age. They might not be steady enough of hand any longer to level a side-arm with reliability, but they were still able to hand out the lamb chops and strawberries with zabaglione at Giovanni's Restaurant, which seemed to serve as a sort of pasture for this particular set of retirees.

What the logistics for this were—who knows? But we were still living in Little Italy the first time we went to Giovanni's with Uncle Edward, and I must have mentioned it to the wholesale pasta guys in the private warehouse where I was allowed to buy De Cecco pasta—this when everyone else in New York was still eating Ronzoni—because one day one of them called to me as I was walking past.

"Hey, sweetheart, you wanna meet Giovanni's son?"

And I was presented to a man in one of those long coats in from New Jersey. "Wine salesman," he told me, and maybe he was. Looking back, I can't believe I asked. Can't believe I kept my neighbors updated on the particulars of my nightlife.

But I was an enthusiast in those days, and in love with the illustrious world I'd just married into, and this man's father, old Mr. Giovanni, was part of that world, and the magic extended to him too, to all of them, standing there in their coats in that dusty warehouse on the corner of Mulberry and Grand, where these guys didn't live anymore, but their mothers still did, which was lucky for me. Because that meant that on the nights when I wasn't dining at eight with Uncle Edward at Giovanni's, I could be walking home alone at three a.m. and there would be no problem, these streets were safe. And that was in New York in the seventies, when you couldn't set foot in the park after six.

Fine, so that was where Giovanni got his waiters, and the surly ones who wouldn't talk to us were still fun to look at, and we soon settled into a routine of dinner there about once a month, alternating with Le Bourguignon on Seventy-Second, which, again, one could die for now, but then was just another very good French place with the additional advantage of being on the ground floor of Uncle Edward's building, where he had moved soon after "your Aunt Kate," as he very sweetly always called her to us, not that we'd ever met her, died.

Horribly, tragically—Uncle Edward told us about it only once. He said that he had come home from his law firm early—it was New Year's Eve—"come home happy," he said, and I can't remember him referring to any other emotion, ever. And then—he passed his hand over his face—he'd found her dead.

Just like that—no sign, no illness, no blood tests, no hair loss, no dreary diminishing. Just a smile in the morning—the smile we'd seen in the one picture we still have. Uncle Edward and Aunt Kate, taken in the forties, I would guess. They are standing together, looking slightly away from the camera. Her hair is done up, but casually, as she must have worn it since she was a schoolgirl, and she is wearing a form-fitting knit dress, very well cut, what we should all be wearing, with her arm through his, and standing very close to him. He has on his suit, as usual, but there is a look on his face that we had never seen. A half smile, with real amusement, exactly matched to hers. They are amused by something off-camera, together, the way it can sometimes be between two people. When they really are, as the service goes, "as one."

Though, almost as an aside, at the very edge of the photo, you can make out the cigarette she is holding in her right hand, which is likely what killed her. Because why else does a tall, good-looking, well-loved woman of fifty-six die just like that, one New Year's Eve afternoon?

It was 1948, say the family records. And there Uncle Edward still would have been, leaving his office early—uncharacteristically, mind you. He was one of those old-fashioned independent New York lawyers, and though there is the persistent family rumor that he went off on his own because he "never made partner," I find this hard to believe.

Especially in light of an anecdote he told us, of how after Adolph Ochs bought the *New York Times*, Uncle Edward had been the one selected by his law firm to find the family a suitable summer place. They had come to New York from Tennessee, where religion wasn't a deal-breaker at the country club, but in Oyster Bay the Ochs children were not welcome at the tennis or sailing. So Uncle Edward, clearly credited with knowing a nice place when he saw one, as well as the right questions to ask and of whom, was given the mission of scouting around, and what he came up with was Lake George, where Adolph Ochs bought the Peabody estate in the late twenties, and where the family has summered from that day to this.

Which must have counted as a strong plus next to Uncle Edward's name at the very least, and if he wasn't in the end a partner at whatever firm it was, maybe the choice was his. Maybe he'd decided he didn't want to work so closely with one group or the other, or maybe he took one of those family dislikes to certain New York types, and withdrew, that sort of thing. Maybe it was political. FDR was in his class at Harvard, and though they knew each other, they hadn't been friends. On the contrary.

But whatever turn his career had taken, Uncle Edward must have made his peace with it by then, because by 1948 he was already sixty-five. And the fact that he'd gone in to work at all on New Year's Eve that year implies both commitment and engagement, even if he had left early that day, with a spring in his step.

On his way home to the woman he still loved despite years of marriage—you can see it in the picture. Home to change from his three-piece suit into his nice old tux and then wait while she slipped into her silks, so they could go wherever it was that they'd planned to go that night, and smile into each other's eyes at midnight, and drink to "the best year ever."

And for him instead to find her lying cold—where? He never said. Bathroom floor, possibly, or bedroom, near the old black telephone? Possibly even with the receiver in her hand?

Not that it mattered. Where she lay, whether she'd fallen with violence or simply in a soft swirl, was nothing to the fact that she was "gone," as people used to say—all at once, gone, like that, with no warning or word of farewell. A live beautiful woman, not young perhaps but still lovely, still the light of someone's life, and then over and out, like that.

"And I came home and found her—" Uncle Edward broke off. Passed his hand over his face. The thirty years from that day to this as nothing.

That night was the end of much for Uncle Edward. After that, he distributed his furniture among his children, excepting, perhaps, the daughter who had become an Episcopal nun and presumably had no need, and moved to the sparsely furnished apartment on East Seventy-Second Street, which had the advantage of sunlight until a high-rise went up directly across the street and blocked it. How was that legal in New York in the seventies? How is it legal now?

Uncle Edward missed the sun, he had taken the apartment for that sun in the morning. But he was too old to consider a move, and there was in that apartment's favor Le Bourguignon, downstairs.

Which was where, most nights, he took his supper, and they knew him well. Knew the lamb chops, unless it was filet of sole. Knew the claret with the former, and the Pouilly-Fuissé with the latter, and the two bourbons on the rocks before either. Knew the precise bare minimum of assistance required to get Uncle Edward to and from the table, and the occasional "into the breach." As one night when we were there with him, he poured the little bowl of butter pats sitting on ice onto his fish, and then called the waiter to complain that the hollandaise was "thin." The waiter apologized and swept away the plate, and was soon back with another. This time I poured the hollandaise.

"Now, that's better," said Uncle Edward with a smile.

A small smile. We were lucky we could get that smile. Get the nostalgic smile as well upon occasion, like the time he told us about when he was a small boy and "Pussy" Wharton, as she was called by her friends, came for tea with his grandmother in Newport. He'd wanted his supper, he said, and Ms. Wharton was staying and staying, so he'd sneaked into the kitchen and rung the dinner bell.

Edith Wharton rose, embarrassed—"I've stayed too long!"—and made a quick exit. Uncle Edward's grandmother swept into the kitchen, furious at the waitress, Christine, for such an infraction. But Uncle Edward fessed up, and so was sent straight to bed without any supper, though Christine sneaked him up some cold pie—another small smile.

But nothing like the one in the picture with Aunt Kate. Strange to think that a smile too can go to the grave, but there it is. Along with one's last youth, the last traces, that is, when suddenly there is no one left who still sees, beyond the wrinkles and the gray and the halting steps on the

stairway, a smooth-cheeked young man who once rowed
for the St. Paul's crew and sailed summers from Newport to
Maine, and then later stood waiting, tall and handsome—
nothing to do with old, no gray, no wrinkles—at the altar in
a small, fashionable church in Washington, to make a vow
that was after all, in the end, kept.

II

"Newton Houghton Can't Come"

IT'S FUNNY, WHEN you're trying to remember, trying to really see it, call it back. There are hardly ever enough photos, and rarely the right ones. And the details of those stories that one holds sharply in one's memory and close to heart, anecdotes related with such vividness that they become, over the years, one's own, are then contradicted, or changed in some profound way in the retelling. An offense, even betrayal, but it happens. Happens all the time, since many of these cherished tales are of a moment, told from a certain corner of an inner cave, colored by the drawings on the wall in that point in space, with the snow howling and a dire wolf at the door.

But the next time one asks, it is springtime, and the teller'd had not dried lichens but roast venison for dinner. The wolf is in the hills, and the needs are other. For him, though not for you, who were never more than passing through anyway.

As with a story, told by and presumably about a relative—Newton was Uncle Edward's middle name—Newton Houghton, whose name, though not particularly striking on paper, actually rhymed in the days when the Boston Houghtons still said "Hoo-tin." The story came from my husband's father, a man whose cold detachment was tempered by his great eye for natural beauty—he had brought home from postwar Japan a passion for bonsai, and had even won first prize in the Philadelphia Flower Show, the real thing, the one that matters most. But he had also waged a lifelong war against certain forms, and once when we were discussing the pros and cons of thank-you notes and RSVPs, he recalled one his mother had received from a cousin, then a half-grown boy who'd clearly been dragged inside and sat down with pen and paper to answer an invitation, and what he wrote was, "Newton Houghton can't come." This, my father-in-law told us, was ever after the great family joke for the ideal regret.

Though when I asked him about it years later, just to hear it again, not only did he have no recollection, but insisted rather testily that he knew of no "Newton Houghton" in the family. And yet, there he sits, if not Newton Houghton then at least my husband's father, clear as anything in my mind's eye, telling the story with his little laugh, in his favorite old red shorts and blue faded shirt, tall icy gin and tonic in hand.

And a cigarette too, from the days when people used to sit, legs crossed, small ashtray balanced on the knee. Cousin Betty, too, used to smoke, she told us, "Chesterfields." That was probably at the beginning of our acquaintance, in the studio apartment we had, up the stairs on West Eighty-Ninth Street, before we were married, the chief attraction of which was a little deck out into the ailanthus trees in the alley behind the brownstones, with a dead stick in a pot when we took the place, in November, and meant to throw out but somehow didn't. And then spring came and the dry stick turned, as if by magic, into a lilac bush and even attracted a bumblebee who dropped by, on its rounds, every evening.

When the bee approached, we developed the habit of falling silent and sitting still, while it buzzed up and down in front of our faces, and then, presumably satisfied, flew into the lilac. Granted this ritual probably owed its origin in some measure to a strong batch of marijuana—too stoned to flee, we'd sat, but weren't stung, since, clearly, we and the bee were on the same wavelength. And so it went, every evening that spring, us, the lilac, and the bee, and the only trouble came once when a visiting friend, also stoned though not into silence, couldn't stop talking, and the bee zoomed in and stung him on the lip.

Which horrified us, more for the sake of the bee, but then we learned that bumblebees don't have to die when they sting, and in fact, it was back the next night, or maybe that was the end of it—it was one of those things. One has no idea that thirty years later, one will be wondering. Caring about something that was, after all, kind of a joke.

But be that as it may, the point is that this was what Cousin Betty was confronting, not to mention the climb up five narrow flights just to get there—we had an idea in those days that the top of the stairs was the place for us to live. No one stomping over our heads, and if that meant climbing untold flights over the years, fine. We were in our twenties, but the first time Betty came, she must have been—well, not so old in retrospect. Fifty-five, maybe, though already introducing herself as our "rather elderly cousin," and it seemed heroic to us—it was heroic—that she would cross the city in those days and climb our steps.

And then there were our dinners, which featured, exclusively, chicken breast with some curry powder stirred into a can of Campbell's mushroom soup, which was then glopped thickly across the whole thing. The recipe had come from a friend, and had seemed like a miracle—"All you have to do is buy the chicken, the curry, and the soup!"—a godsend, because who knew how to cook in those days? Other nights it might be boiled noodles or Mexican TV dinners, but here was something presentable that one could reliably make and serve, and serve we did, though no one who came to us for dinner more than a few times has likely gone near curried chicken since. I know we never have.

And it all would have been particularly hard on Betty, since she herself was a true gourmet cook, the very first and best we had ever met. If it was chicken with her, it would have been coq au vin, although what we dream of still are her lovely little roasts with mushroom sauces and perfect tiny vegetables arranged all around—one of which we particularly remember because it was one of those nights when someone, Betty in this case, invites a "nice young couple" for you to meet, and you have already taken a definitive dislike to each other even before the door has clicked shut behind you.

Nor have we ever forgotten that couple. First we politely argued our way through cocktails, with the man defending, in the name of science, Allied Chemical's right to continue dumping Kepone into the James River until scientists "prove" it causes kidney cancer in people and not just six thousand white rats—with poor Betty, every time one of us took a breath, valiantly steering the conversation back to the weather: "hot!" or "cold!" though by then we were disagreeing on that. And then, at last, as we were moving to the table for our reward, only then did they mention that they had recently become vegetarians. They hadn't wanted to give extra trouble, they said, by bringing it up before.

Then why bring it up now? I wanted to pick up a salad fork and prick the man's skinny arm. He should eat meat, maybe that was his problem. They were divinity students too, both of them, and thus felt the pain of the three of us left with plates of nothing but brown meat, since the two of them had to be given all the beautifully glazed carrots and onions and small red potatoes, just then in season.

"Can vegetarians have chocolate?" I couldn't stop myself from asking them, as the pots de crème came out of the kitchen. "Isn't it something to do with animals? The cream?"

And we could see them wavering, not quite sure how much further they were now obliged to go; wondering if perhaps they shouldn't, in penance for the unfortunate, though clearly foreseeable, turn of events at dinner, deprive themselves of the dessert. But those little pots, with the darkest of chocolate and the crème baked in the center, were beyond any human's poor powers of resistance. Which brings me to a further point, much more of the essence than the fact that those two short-term, long-lapsed, as-vegetarian-as-my-Labrador-dog future Episcopal priests of course ate those desserts that night: the kitchen out of which those pots de crème were produced. Cousin Betty's kitchen.

"No, no, NO!" Betty's voice would rise, to desperate levels, if any one of us, trying to be helpful, so much as approached the kitchen. She wanted no help, she insisted. Help, to her, was to stay away from the kitchen. She wanted no witnesses, no killjoys, no snoops, no one to draw back the curtain on the miracles that she was performing there. Managing to get such dinners out of such a kitchen.

Because it was miserable, that kitchen, a sort of galley,

dark and tiny, though not out of place in the walk-up flat on the dingy part of First Avenue where Cousin Betty had landed. Though, once inside, you could, excepting the kitchen, forget that you'd entered through a metal door with peeling paint, and climbed a flight or two of grimy stairs, always avoiding the squashed cockroach here or there. But as soon as you entered her door, there were the last of the Queen Anne chairs from her mother's house, creating their own world, and the stiff little sofa that had once stood to the side of a sitting room.

Rickety, all of them, and once the dining room table actually collapsed mid-supper, drenching half of us with the good red wine that Betty had produced for that evening—but most of the time, if you sat quietly and still, all was well, and you were far from First Avenue.

In fact, you were almost back in Plainfield, New Jersey, circa 1920, where Betty had grown up, on a hill off a street lined with grand old maples and horse chestnuts standing tall, in a nice big house filled with furniture of this sort, but still solid, in its heyday. Her father was a successful patent lawyer, and there were servants and a tennis court at home, along with the great-grandmother's house in Newport, and a family compound in Vermont. We have a photo of Betty there, when she was about sixteen, at a family wedding, looking beautiful, ethereal, thin, and blond. Her father was still alive then, tall and cross-looking—for this was his wife's family, not his—and somewhat familiar as well, since we all know the face of his son, Betty's brother, whom we called "Cousin Archie," and who came to personify the gravitas of the law vs. Nixon during the darkest of the Watergate days.

But the future special prosecutor is still a schoolboy

in this picture, probably a senior at St. Paul's or maybe a freshman at Harvard, and quite good-looking, with a shock of blond hair in the front, before the days of his signature crew cut. And there was Cousin Molly as well, their little sister, her lovely dark hair set off by a ribbon, still in small girl's clothes, a white dress with a sash, pink or blue. And Russell too, their cousin and ours, a little boy, in the front with the rest of them, in short pants and little white socks. So the whole guest list of our dinner this night was there, because Uncle Edward is standing in the back, dark-haired and also glowering, so maybe everyone was cross, maybe it was hot in Vermont that day. Or maybe the photographer dallied, or maybe even it was that some of the party were already sensing those terrible losses that would soon be crashing down on some of them—most of them—before long.

Betty must have been a schoolgirl in the picture, but I can't remember her ever saying where she'd gone to school. Her brothers we know about—all the men in the family went to St. Paul's and Harvard, which was, by the way, no big deal in those days in those circles. Simply where they went. No one was overly excited about it.

But the girls—where did the girls go? Nowhere in particular, or I think I would have remembered. You might suppose they'd have been sent, alongside their brothers, over to Farmington or down to St. Tim's, and then on to Smith or Vassar. But I don't think they were, nor in her day was their mother, one of the Frances Perkinses of the family, called Fanny—she too is a beautiful child, in an earlier photo, taken on the steps of a grand house somewhere, a generation earlier. Family lore has it that she was sighted by Betty's father coming out of her parents' house when she was seven years old, and claimed, on the spot, as "the girl I'm going to marry." He, the future father, was twenty-five at the time.

Which sounds less like sunny America circa 1900 than Grimm's dark woods, or actually, late eighteenth century Electorate of Saxony, where the poet Novalis also spotted a child, as she turned from a window. His future wife, he declared her, and courted her throughout her entire growing up, and that's who she was, all her conscious life after that—Novalis's fiancée. His "Philosophy," he called her, making a play on her name, "Sophie," which she likely never understood, since her ties to the poet gave her a special status in the schoolroom, and no one could make her do her lessons after that. It was said that she wouldn't read and couldn't write.

Which ended up not mattering, since she caught TB and died just as she was turning fifteen, before the marriage could take place.

But in Aunt Fanny's case, as we would eventually come to call the small girl on the American steps that day, the fantasy played itself out, and she was married at seventeen, happily, it is said. There were lots of charming stories, and seven children—five of whom, the boys, went on to head distinguished schools and challenge Presidents, and the other two were the girls, who were brought up to marry well, which was how their lives were supposed to work out.

And Betty did, if not well, at least marry. It was before World War II, in the late thirties. He was probably someone who knew her brothers and had been to Harvard, which might have been how she met him. There is, however, a small chance that since she was enrolled at that time at the Art Students League in New York, studying sculpture, he might have been a rogue from the start, lurking around the place, looking for pretty art types.

At any rate, she fell in love with him, and there must have been some obstacles to the match, because she once told me that she'd read all of Gibbon when she was "waiting to marry John. It was partly for him, to tease him, and partly for me, and partly it grew and became a superstition, to bring my marriage to John about."

Pure Betty, that; high Betty—just how she would tease a man. And it worked in the end, the marriage did take place, though why it had to be "brought about" is now the question. Was her heart's desire—because he must have been that, surely, to read Gibbon for—in some way "inappropriate," as we say, or just hesitant? Was it her family who put up the barriers, or was there a prophetic wavering on his part? He was, after all, a lawyer by then, so would have had prospects; though all an elderly cousin could remember about him was that "he'd had to take the bar twice."

Which must have been memorable in those days, and in that family, though there might have been a good explanation for his want of diligence to the law. Because it turned out that "Betty's John," as they came to call him, saw himself less as a lawyer than as a future famous author of detective novels, and there is the nagging question of whether this was where Betty came into his scheme. Her uncle was, at that time, editing Hemingway and Fitzgerald for Scribner's. Mightn't this key editor's gaze be more likely drawn to one new detective novel among the scrum if the author was known to him, married to his niece?

It turned out it was, or at least that the book was in fact published by Scribner's, in 1940. Betty once loaned me her copy. "New York Bohemiana," read the blurb on the back, where "a young sculptress is found murdered in her room."

"That's me," she said with a smile.

A different smile from her usual self-effacement, compounded over years, I supposed, of courage and disappointment, mixed. This one was almost girlish, with a touch of real delight. Harking back to the "New York Bohemiana" that she must have been living then. Which must have been, then as now, fun.

So there had been at least that, in her trajectory. A choice that, however it turned out, had sprung from high hopes.

Not that one is exactly choosing at the young ages when paths like that are taken, without any respect for consequences. All you can really think at nineteen is that you no longer want to live in a big white house with green shutters in Plainfield, New Jersey. That you were born for more than playing wife to a patent attorney, or mother to his seven children.

But what do you really know, when you toss your head and insist on a man who is also chafing at the bit? Who hasn't passed his bar exam, but you don't care because what he really is, is a great writer, and what you yourself are is an artist too, a sculptor but not of weekend modeling clay.

No, a real sculptor who will marry a real writer, no matter what the family thinks, and who does precisely that, with a shy and delighted smile, and absolutely no understanding, no way of understanding what every single member of that wedding party over the age of fifty knew: that that path would lead eventually, through a predictable series of permutations and combinations that did in fact play out, to some version of Betty's bad flat on First Avenue, paid for painfully, month to month, out of meager wages earned correcting grammatical barbarisms in run-of-the-mill children's books at a diminishing press.

And clinging finally, with or without bitterness—this we never knew—to the last remnants of the house in Plainfield after all. Never stooping once to mention the servants or tennis court, but taking great care of the last of the chairs as her sole witnesses. Family retainers almost, mute, and decrepit now, true, but they had been there. They had seen her then.

"I wasn't sure what to think," she said that night to us, when she showed us her ex-husband's book, "when he killed me off"—but anyway, there were two children by then, by the time the book was finally published, though it didn't, in the end, fulfill their expectations, hers and his; did not establish her husband alongside the other writers her uncle was publishing that year.

And soon after that, World War II broke out, and Betty's John enlisted, not that he had to. Since he was already in his thirties, and the father of two, as well as a lawyer and a writer, and there were plenty of other ways for him to serve. But he was all for going, which Betty took for nobility, patriotism, and so he went, to Europe. But when the war finally ended, and the shiploads and shiploads of soldiers and sailors came thundering down the gangplanks in New York Harbor into delirious waiting arms, Betty's John turned out to be not among them.

Betty never spoke of it, except once, when we were talking about Proust. She had read him, she said, in Las Vegas, while waiting to get her divorce from John. When he didn't come back after the war, she had held her breath for as long as she could, without pressing, although she must have sensed something was amiss. He was still writing letters, still offering excuses for a year or so, so she could still believe him when he claimed that in all the confusion over there, there was much work left to be done. Especially since he'd learned colloquial German, his country needed him there, and he felt obliged to walk this extra mile, though it prevented him from coming home to his wife and his children, which he would do as soon as he'd fulfilled his duty, and so on.

But the letters dwindled, and eventually stopped, and it had to be faced that no matter how patient and understanding one was, no matter how long and faithfully one waited, there might be no homecoming after all. And then it turned out there was a German woman, had been for some time, a wife in deed if not on paper, Betty was finally apprised. This in the days when divorce in New York barely existed without detectives, sordid photos, lipstick on collars—"grounds."

But there was Las Vegas, and that was where this Bohemian reader of Gibbon went, on the Greyhound bus, but this time with Proust, the seven volumes filling the dark green leather case she'd been given by her Philadelphia aunt as part of her wedding trousseau. It seemed an affront—she'd almost cried out, to see her fine English case tossed under the bus along with the battered cardboard and cloth ragtag pertaining to the rest of the passengers, but there it was. And there she was. On her way to Las Vegas to fulfill the six-week residency that was required then for a Nevada divorce, with nothing between her and the deadbeats, the floozies, and the sharpsters on the bus beside her but the Proust.

Though it proved to be, in its way, enough. Gave her the

cover to face her mother, her brothers, her New York friends—
"I'm going to Las Vegas for six weeks to read Proust!"

And, "Betty!" they could exclaim, instead of, "Poor
Betty." "That Betty!" which was to say, still Betty, despite
this blow. Opening with the English and closing with the
French—so there it was still, her lovely good humor, that
trace of high spirits, though he'd taken much from her,
her deadbeat husband. But he hadn't taken everything,
clearly. Betty.

And her Proust served her in Vegas as well, erected
a stout wall all around her. And it's tempting, flicking
through those early, high-contrast Kodachrome color shots
of the Hotel Apache or Flamingo in the late forties, when
Betty was there and it was so easy to be bad, so clean, compared to what followed, to wish her just one short sidestep
from her Proust into, say, Raymond Chandler, who might
have intrigued her. Unsettled her enough to lift her eyes
to the window and get her outside one fresh morning onto
what wasn't quite the Strip yet, and into a little shop where
a gum-cracking bleached blonde would call her Sugar and
sell her a one-piece navy-blue swimsuit piped with white.

And then who knows what might not have happened?
Because she would have looked good to a jaded eye out
there, would have looked almost like a visitation to a studio head or rum-running banker with a showgirl by his
side, who thought he'd seen it all when it came to women,
but had never seen anything remotely like Betty. The tall,
thin, aristocratic frame. The hair, no longer blond but
once blond. Truly blond, with even the fade signifying the
real thing.

And Las Vegas was as well known for its marriage cha-
pels as its divorce courts, and it would have answered, in

its way, would have spoken even louder to the tuned ears back home than the Proust did. But though it's intriguing to imagine Betty taking "New York Bohemiana" to the next level, beyond the pale really, and marrying a millionaire, moving to California, what really happened was what they call "No dice" out there. There was no look out any Las Vegas windows, those true blue eyes never did lift and look west. There would be no bungalow in the palms off Sycamore Drive for her, no case-study house high in the Hollywood Hills. California—even one where she could have transformed herself, her fall, into a local triumph and actually started a new life—was never on the table. That low she had not fallen.

And lest there remain any trace of doubt, lest any of the more forward among her fellows there, the taut, tough gals in tight capri pants, and the men in their powder-blue, shirts open at the throat, and all those chains around their necks, *mon dieu*—should any newcomer among them, for they were constantly replenishing themselves, consider a foray, with the suggestion of a highball or a look-see visit to the Pair-O-Dice, there was the citadel of cultured Europe against them, Volumes I, II, III, IV, V, VI, and finally VII, firmly before her, propped against her single glass of iced tea with the long tall silver spoon she'd brought from home, at the small table, where she sat both morning and evening, alone.

And when it was over, when she hopped the Dog back to New York, campaign completed, what did she read then? What would have helped? Austen for the courage? H. James for the company?

Because she would have needed both courage and company of that magnitude, since no one got divorced in those days. She would be the only divorcée—horrid word—they knew. The children would be the only ones in school, if they could even stay in school. That was another question.

And how that was resolved we never heard, nor the details of what must have been a steadily downward progression of moves, from wherever they were living in 1941, when the breadwinner of the family sallied off to war, all the way to First Avenue, where Betty had touched down when we knew her, in the seventies. Her children were long married themselves, living in some pleasant suburbs, as close a version of their grandmother's Plainfield as they could manage. They'd had enough of "New York Bohemiana" by then.

The first time I heard Betty's voice—cultured, slightly breathy, and unmistakable ever after—was on the telephone. She was the one who had called, but she was so hesitant on the phone, so almost dithering, that I nearly hung up, taking her for a crank. I would come to learn that she—actually all of them, the whole family, all the siblings and cousins—treated the telephone as suspect, a modern intrusion that could be accepted but never embraced.

"Hello," they would say, "I'm calling on the telephone," or something equally absurd on the face of it, but in fact code for, *I trust you know that I know I should be writing instead, or leaving my card, but here we are, in the world as it is, adapting, all of us, what else can we do?*

And the proper answer was enough of a fluster on one's own end to convey both acquaintance with the code and sufficient lack of ease to indicate at least some breeding. Although looking back, the seventies were probably the high-water mark of actually talking to someone on the phone, since answering machines had yet to go mainstream. The only one we knew who had one then was Marty the Seltzer Man, who would sing an adapted version of "Love Potion No. 9," and then instruct you to leave a message "at the sound of seltzer splashing." That's how it was in those days.

"Yes, yes, hello?" Betty finally managed, that first time she called, when I answered instead of my husband, or still boyfriend in those days, which had probably added to the fluster. And then she said something about being "rather elderly."

"Is this Cousin Betty, then?" I asked, hoping I sounded sufficiently tentative on my end. Not that I could match them, ever.

"Yes," she said, "I'm afraid it is."

III

"You Better Take That Diamond Ring, You Better Pawn It, Babe"

AND IT WOULD have been Betty, the key to it all, to the family, the elder sister still and always, undeposed from that, despite what the world had done to her—Betty would have been the first one we'd have called to invite the night Uncle Edward was coming to dinner. Because without her, nothing was possible—so probably we called her first, and she would have arrived, as she always did, *à l'heure*, but she was not the first one to ring the bell that evening, nor was it Uncle Edward, at eight o'clock sharp.

There was a ring sometime around a quarter to, and I, dressed, thank goodness, went down, opened the door, and found myself standing, face-to-face, with what we used to call a bum from the street, complete with lank and greasy hair hanging in her face, and ill-fitting, wrinkled clothes in no way approximating clean.

I stared.

"Hullo," said a distinctive, aristocratic voice.

I realized it was Betty's sister, Molly, and though there are details I forget about the evening, I can still distinctly remember standing there, telling myself, *It's all right, she*

lives somewhere nearby, and since she probably hates the tele-
phone too, she's just stopped by after what must have been a very
hard day at work, to say that she's on her way home to wash up
and change and would be a bit late.

So sure was I that this was her intention, had to be her
intention—she couldn't possibly expect to come in like that,
not only looking but smelling—that I didn't even ask her in
at first, just stood there with an anticipatory smile, waiting
for her to finish her excuses and trot off.

But she made no excuses. Simply stood there in the door-
way, with that lovely gentle smile they all have, lips closed,
very pink, very nice, from their mother. "I'm afraid I'm a bit
early?" She smiled.

She'd come directly from work, she said. She was an X-
ray technician up at Columbia—we would learn later how
respected she was up there, how beloved.

"No, no, not at all," I must have said then, though still
in disbelief—had she *really* come to dinner like that? What
was she *thinking*? And worse, what would Uncle Edward
think?

Wouldn't he be appalled, or possibly insulted, at the
very least distressed? He who had known her in those
lawn dresses with blue satin sashes, and there was another
photo I saw recently, which made the whole thing even
worse—Molly with her mother and her brothers and sister Betty, and all of them lovely beyond words, like some
vision of an American Camelot, but real, there that day, to
be caught on film. They are ranged in chairs on the lawn,
with good old trees behind them, dogwood in bloom, and
maples towering overhead. The big boys are in neckties,
the future head of Groton in short pants, and Aunt Fanny
is still beautiful, still grand and firm, holding down the

middle. But the girls—my God! Betty is eighteen or so, and thin enough for a Paris runway. Her hair is cut short, like the girls in her uncle's authors' new books, and her two-piece knit is already saying New York. She is posing, a bit, but Molly isn't posing. She looks straight into the camera, direct, with a wry and slightly amused look in her eyes.

She must have been about fourteen then, in a linen dress with covered buttons and a little cardigan. If you had to predict her future from this, you might have said "academic," or possibly "poet." "Wife of a poet," at the very least. "President of Bryn Mawr."

Which somehow rang a distant bell, kindled a small hope, and I actually called Bryn Mawr College recently, thinking that maybe there was a chance.

But no, said the alumnae people. Molly's name was not on any of their lists.

"Maybe she didn't graduate?"

Even if she hadn't, they said.

But what then? What did she do instead? How did she get from covered buttons on that lawn to the stained Dacron skirt and pilled black jersey that she showed up in that night? Shortly after the Camelot photograph, in 1930, just as the Depression was setting its teeth, their father died of lung cancer, at age fifty-six. And shortly after that, the servants were let go, and Aunt Fanny had to pay a call on the rector of St. Paul's School to beg a scholarship for the next brother in line, so that he could be sent.

A hard call, that one, but it got worse, got to the point where the proverbial boarders had to be taken in to the big

white house on the hill, but despite that, the boys in the picture that day all did fine. Combining Horatio Alger's ringing
virtues of "honesty, thrift, self-reliance, industry, a cheerful
whistle and an open manly face," they took summer jobs,
moved to less expensive rooms at college, disdained frivol-
ity, and conquered the world, each in his own way.

But the girls—in particular Molly, to whom also pertained the "honesty, thrift, self-reliance, industry, cheerful
whistle" and "open" if not manly "face," why was there no
less-expensive dorm room for her to move into? No scholarship request from her mother to any school at all?

Not that a lesser education would have handicapped
her in the marriage field, at that point; in fact, it might
have given an advantage to a girl like that—with a gaze
already on the direct side. A smile with nothing of the
flirtatious about it. But what if you don't necessarily
see yourself sitting in the middle of the picture, twenty
years down the road, anchoring a brood of your own?
What if the very thought makes you weak in the knees?
Almost queasy?

What then, with no degree, no mentors, no examples?

Nowhere to turn, in fact. In slightly older days, a "maiden
sister" would have moved in with one of her brothers—whoever had the biggest household and most tolerable wife—
and helped with the mending. Once it became clear that
she would remain among the un-paired, and it wouldn't do
for them to have her taking in washing.

But those days were over. Which meant that an "honest,
self-reliant" girl like Molly would have grown up facing the
fact that her income would have to be in her own hands—or
maybe it didn't happen that way at all. Maybe she thought
for some time, too long, that there would be someone for

her, someone she liked, who would someday look at her and like her back. That among the scores of young men who passed through their lives, there would be one—one of her brother's friends—who would turn to her. "What were you saying, Molly?"

Turn and look at her clear eyes—not her well-ironed shirtwaist and nicely combed hair, bespeaking possible wifely virtues. Because when the badminton started, the dress would get wrinkled and the hair come undone, as she played to win. So not wifely after all, but couldn't she have expected that among them all, there would be one who would ask what she was saying? What she was reading, even. That there would be someone in this whole wide world who would ask.

And it doesn't seem such an entirely impossible dream, that there would be one interesting, slightly offbeat young man, among the golden youth her brothers were bringing home all the years of her metamorphosis. A Leonard Woolf. Even someone like her youngest brother, who married a slightly frazzled woman who was a lawyer herself. So Molly could have still been waiting, as it came upon her by degrees, her unmarried-ness, with nothing definitive about it at first, until it was too late for her to be one of those bold, committed, lone-wolf women in med school; you can see how the question of what to do with herself when she first left the house in Plainfield might not have been taken too seriously.

She would have gone naturally to New York, and it does seem odd that she didn't ask her uncle for a job. As an editorial assistant of some sort. Surely she knew how to type? Or could have gotten someone to front her the tuition for a quick course at Katy Gibbs, the secretarial school populated with all those waves of female graduates of any and every university and college in the country, the ones who wanted or needed jobs. It couldn't have been expensive then—it wasn't even expensive in the early seventies, when the last of us were still limping in—and surely someone could have paid for Molly?

Even one of her brothers by then, but maybe people just don't do that. After all, her own mother had been permitted to take in boarders, and there is even a description of her, by one of her son's Harvard roommates, "running about, with her hair flying wild," which makes it all sound like good scattershot fun, and she would have wanted it that way.

But how much of a joke was it, really, to the mother, Aunt Fanny, and especially to her younger daughter, who would have still been at home then, and by necessity part of the "running about"? Because there would have been laundry and cooking and cleaning with all the scrub brushes and scouring pads and mops that that still entailed in those days, and not just for the boarders but for two younger brothers as well. And Molly must have noted that despite all this, her mother made no appeal for help, not even to her own brother who lived in real splendor in the countryside outside of Philadelphia.

But it was his wife's money—there didn't seem to be anything from the old family fortune left for Aunt Fanny or her siblings. They were just one generation too far removed.

Their grandfather had paid her brothers' club dues at Harvard—including Uncle Edward's—but their mother, also widowed young, had been forced to spend principal. There were still the tales of the palazzos in Florence and Michelangelos on their grandmother's walls, but no one in the family was dining out on that any longer. In fact, they never spoke of it at all.

It didn't occur to us to ask Molly what she did, exactly. It seemed both indelicate and also something that we somehow should have known. Might have been told sometime when we weren't properly listening. Because it is only now that one cares sharply, when there is no one left to ask.

What we did know was that she worked up at Columbia, in the hospital, but not as a doctor. A technician, but this was nothing—in any family discussion of Molly—to the whisper that she drank. That was what one was told at the time—"She drinks." Followed by nods. Head shakes. A sigh.

Single women, Jane Austen noted in the early 1800s, have "a dreadful propensity for being poor." And there was Molly that night, at the door, a twentieth century version of perhaps Elinor, or even Marianne, for that matter, though without the benefit of Austen's wizard endings, so still unmarried, still poor.

"She drinks." Yes, thank God she drank—it's the best one could wish her, if you just step back a bit. Given that she wasn't one to take up folk dancing or answer personals in the back of the *New York Review* from an "SWM" seeking "SWF." Impossible, the logistics of it, the meeting, the pathos, the degradation. Nor was there any possibility, with that clear straight gaze one knows from that picture, of some pleasant and effective diversion, a "project," a biography, perhaps, as someone in the family had once suggested, of her great-grandfather, Charles C. Perkins, born in Florence, chief donor to and founder of the Boston Museum of

Fine Arts less than a century ago, whose papers would be, it was pointed out, accessible to her.

But no, not for Molly. Just the thought made her reach for her bourbon. Pour two glasses at once, ha ha, show them, those feigning, fawning fools, stuck in the past, but here was the future. Two days in front of her, Saturday and Sunday, the Empty Quarter, and she no less than Lawrence, T. E., of Arabia, having to trudge across, only with no boy, so more so, alone, *totallement* alone, and not just once, like Lawrence, who arrived to a hero's welcome, but every week of the year. Every single Friday, when she walked with no ado—Lawrence had made a fuss—out of the hospital where she worked with people she knew, you might almost call them friends, only none of them ever asked her to dinner or even coffee over the weekend, ever— but they seemed like, and even, in their way, were friends there, inside, but when they walked out, even sometimes together, still it had already started. Her fraught and solitary trek.

Not that they knew it, of course, for one never said nothin'—ha ha. That's how she talked sometimes, in the desert. "As bad as I want to be," she would tell herself as she left the subway station, the last outpost, but how bad did she want to be? That was the problem. Because she didn't want to be bad, she wanted to be good, just not stupid. Not compromised. Not dishonest. Not somebody's wife, maybe, but did that automatically entail trudging alone through it all for so much of her life—her life?

And sometimes there would be Betty and her girls, or Russell, or for a while her mother, who, being an obligation, was easier somehow, especially as all other socializing started proving first burdensome and then, finally, impossible. Almost.

But she could still take the train to Plainfield some Saturday mornings in decent weather, where things had righted themselves a bit as her brothers established themselves and put in some money. So no more boarders, and if the old house was falling quietly to pieces around them, Molly didn't mind that, *au contraire*. She would have been shaken, upended, by any "improvements."

And there were the tall trees and the high, uncut lawn which had turned imperceptibly to meadow, filled with speedwell and the dandelions it used to be her job to dig out in the spring. She remembered the neighbor's Italian gardener used to come by sometimes and ask for the greens, which was fine with them. "Weeds to us," her mother would say, smiling almost apologetically.

Her mother, young then. Molly too. Well, now she saw dandelion greens for sale in the greengrocers, but never thought to pick the ones on what they still called the lawn. *Eat the dandelions? Surely you jest*, said a voice in her ear, though whose she couldn't imagine, certainly not hers or her mother's. They had read *Stalking the Wild Asparagus* aloud one weekend, and both loved it. But then her mother had fallen asleep, and Molly was alone again, the night was young, which was to say, would stretch on and on, until it was old and everything itched and rubbed and bothered, and there was no bourbon in the house, only the last of someone's Canadian Club—could it have been her father's? From the thirties? That, and a half bottle of sweet sherry, which in the end made her very sick.

And then she'd had to deal with the empty bottles, like a bad girl, which she was, she guessed—what else was she?

Hadn't she disappointed her mother, her brothers, Betty too, all of them? She would sleep in her old bed, and dream that she had slept through a breakfast date with her father and her dead brother, and missed a play, scheduled, somehow, after the breakfast. She had meant to go, they had tickets for her, they were waiting, but she had drawn the curtains in her room, pulled the blinds, and overslept.

She would wake in a sweat in tears, and take an early train back. It was Sunday by then, anyway. When she got back to the city, she would be just one of many, anyone, married with children even—a harried materfamilias crowding into the market on a Sunday afternoon.

But on the whole, those visits to her mother had offered some relief, until the house was sold and her mother moved up to Vermont, which meant no weekends, but still solved Thanksgiving and Christmas, until it no longer did. Why dwell on it? Any of it? And once even the invitations she shrank from stopped coming—one brother had moved to England, another's children had chicken pox, and then were grown and having their own Thanksgivings, to which their parents but not their problematic aunt were invited—then she found herself with yet another windswept plain to struggle across. Colder, actually, "blizzard conditions," only natural given the time of year, of course, but made worse by all the insane cheerfulness that took hold of the whole city. Everyone crying, "Merry Christmas!" every time you bought so much as a cigarette or an old-fashioned, until you got downtown and walked east till it calmed down, once you got to the Bowery and then ground to a final halt on Chrystie Street, where the all-night girls had nothing Merry Christmas about them, and the bums and junkies lay half-frozen in the gutters and held their peace.

She was actually the cheerful one there, had to stop herself singing out, *"Feliz Navidad!"* to one of the pimps as he
slipped down an alley. Funny, how that worked, how once
she was clear of it, she sometimes found herself reverting
to type. Once she even resolved to make a little feast for
herself, nothing to do with Pilgrims or Indians, though! It
would be Stroganoff and her favorite, Floating Island.

But when she pulled down her mother's old cookbook
and blew off the dust, she found it had coffee for twenty,
but not really Floating Island for one. "Serves twelve"—sixteen eggs, so for one? One and a half? How do you split an
egg? Like a half cup of tea? Ha ha. She ripped out the page
and tore it into very small pieces, which she threw up in the
air like confetti, so it turned out to be a celebration after all,
but that only came to her later, once the bourbon kicked in.

And still she managed to smile at me that night in the door-
way, in that way that said there were times when nothing
much had changed, not fundamentally. She was early, she
said, because she was very much afraid of being late for
Uncle Edward. She was particularly happy to be seeing
him again. He had been terribly nice to her once, when she
was a child and had gotten sick on a train—she mentioned
it twice. And I remember wondering if it was that no one
else had ever been nice to her. Or that Uncle Edward was,
as I had heard, rarely nice to anyone, and that this special
treatment had shed a lasting grace on them both.

IV

A Solid Aluminum Donkey

I CAN'T REMEMBER what we drank that night before dinner. We must have had bourbon, because that was Uncle Edward's drink, but what else did we drink in those years before Prosecco and tequila? We'd moved beyond our rum-and-Coke days—all those metal stalls with all that throw-up—and martinis were still just people's parents being boring on the terrace. My husband had recently found a bottle of ancient Rainwater in his grandmother's cellar, so maybe Betty and I sipped that, but I can't imagine Molly thinking Madeira would beat a bourbon and soda, or even a bourbon on the rocks, or, lacking ice, straight up.

And I still wonder where we sat in that apartment. It was a sweet place, with two marble fireplaces, but not much in the way of furniture. We'd been given some nice family pieces when we got married, which had sailed right into storage, including the grand old bed, because who wanted to sleep in a bed in those days? Not when there were suddenly futons in the world.

But I remember a portable rattan sofa, hopefully with some pillows, looking out over the courtyard in the back. I know this was where we sat before dinner, because everyone in the family, one by one, as they came in, from Uncle Edward down, mentioned and identified an unusual tree just out the window. A corkscrew willow, "a sport," as Uncle Edward called it.

"A sport of nature," said Russell, catching sight of it as he came in that evening, also early, since he too, though in his fifties, was still scared of being late for Uncle Edward.

"I think Russell was wearing a Chinese jacket that night," I said recently to an in-law, who vehemently denied the possibility. And though I couldn't swear to it, that is how I see him—essentially Bohemian. But it might not have been a Chinese jacket, it might have been a tweed relic from Brooks Brothers, with even a tie. Oddly enough, though I saw him fairly often, I can't picture him clearly anymore.

Who I see clearly is his father, a terrifying shade still stalking the edges of the family consciousness. He's the one you see first in all the family pictures, where he always strikes a noble pose, profile turned to the camera. And indeed, with his pointed beard and his hand in his jacket, he is the picture of dash and romance, and though his wife, Russell's mother, another Mary called Molly, wasn't beautiful, she was described as "handsome," which meant large and strong, with a high, round brow. Good-looking, but nothing glamorous about her, nothing dramatic in her gentle smile.

Russell's forebears here are dressed as well as anyone else, and his siblings too, so was this before the fateful trip to England? Or France, or both, since Russell's father had staked all on his definitive biography of Benjamin Franklin, which at that time still remained to be written. And for which he relinquished what we would call a tenure-track teaching position at Harvard, and dragged the whole household across the sea, for Franklin had spent time in both Paris and London, and there were troves there yet to be researched. Russell's father would be the first.

And whatever money there was went into this project, was invested in this project, solidly, Russell's family believed and had every right to believe. And the work progressed, and was completed at last, and shipped under separate cover—how? why? my God, what were they thinking?—back to Cambridge, Mass., whence the family also returned.

To wait. Russell's father's first inquiries to the shipping office somewhere down near the Boston Harbor would not have been frantic. For a few weeks, one can see how he would have been able to fully accept a clerk's account of storms off Gibraltar or traffic in Southampton; could have gone home to his wife with growing annoyance but no overweening fear. "It has been delayed."

But there would have come the day when a more senior clerk would have emerged from the back office with reassurances and talk of an official search. And from there, it would have gone the way it does in such cases, with apologies eventually replacing the excuses, once Russell's father's manuscript, of which he had no copies—people didn't in those days—was declared officially lost.

And here is where we look away, so as not to have to watch the light go out in those lively eyes, or the hand pass in front of that noble face, not, that day, in profile. Perhaps it took some time to sink in. Hope, that "subtle Glutton," might have fed awhile longer upon those Fair— and even as I write this, I confess to wondering if I should sell a rug and run over to Italy, the last place, apparently, that Thomas Head Thomas's *Life of Franklin* was traced. Because who throws out a manuscript, even if you're stealing the nice leather case in which it's packed? Wouldn't even a thief have stuffed it under a bed somewhere, or a loose floorboard in a chapel to Our Lady of Lost Causes? Just for luck?

And in those days, it wasn't so easy to dispose of so much paper, and so on, I find myself thinking—and this is eighty years later, so one can imagine how it was for them then, with the vision of the thing itself still shimmering, almost within reach. But finally, there would have dawned for them all, perhaps sequentially, in order of birth, the day when they would have had to face the new fact of their lives: that their father's great work had vanished into the maw.

A terrible blow, that, and it must have felt like a singular misfortune, though as the Russians say, have to say, so often they've got it down to one word, "It happens." It happened to Lawrence of Arabia—someone walked off with the case holding his completed manuscript of *Seven Pillars of Wisdom* in Reading Station, and he somehow had it in him to write it again.

But his book was in his head, and Russell's father's book was based on all that research in all those libraries. Plus Lawrence didn't have a wife and children still looking up every time he walked in the door, with hope still writ on their faces—all those faces, five children, and the handsome wife—well after his own hopes had given way to despair. They had been proud of him. Their father was a great man, doing something big, and as far as they were concerned, the lost pages had been as good as printed on creamy paper and bound in vellum. Had practically already found their place on the family shelves, somewhere between Carlyle and their great-grandfather's *Tuscan Sculptors*.

Almost—but not. Not yet, or not ever? It would have been something for the children to grapple with, that immensity. And they surely would have continued to hope the longest, not necessarily for the original miracle—though there must have lived in their small hearts the off chance that the clerk was wrong after all, and the great pages would turn up one day when they least expected, that fairy-tale day when they hadn't remembered to think about it even once.

But once that was outgrown, who wouldn't have continued to hope that their father would still strike back at his harsh fate, not with a sword but with his pen? And if he'd just sat down then and re-created even a slim volume, even the most memorable parts that still must have been fresh in his mind, then at least they'd all have had that.

But Russell's father was not the man for the slim volume. The whole venture had been based on the "definitive version." That was what had justified it to begin with, the use of his money, his wife's money, all that money, and now there was no more money to bankroll a rewrite of scale, so in the end, there was nothing.

Or maybe he tried. Maybe he sat evenings in a local library, pen in hand, and tried, hard, to call back what had slipped away. Or walked by shipping agencies, studying the windows for off-season rates, because wasn't God in the details? And weren't the details over there, across the sea, and now out of reach?

Who knows? By the time the story came down to us, it had regularized itself into an archetypal morality tale. A man who could have done well for himself, had the background, the education, but squandered it all on a dream, an illusion. The grasshopper in winter. A house of straw. A father good for little beyond the profile turned artfully—artists!—in the family portraits for the occasional photographer, whom he would never be the one to pay.

Still, "we beat on," as one of his uncle's authors was writing around then, "boats against the current." Russell was the youngest, an "afterthought," a cousin told us. His father went back to teaching—at Harvard, presumably, since they lived in Cambridge, though he's not on their updated lists of distinguished professors. But we all know what Harvard is these days. Billionaire central. Very different crowd. They've tossed their gentler poets down the stairs.

And speaking of poets, I heard only after his death that Russell had published a collection of poems featuring, we were told, a "solid aluminum donkey." Though once we got ahold of the book online, it turned out the donkey was "luminous," not aluminum, but no less strange for that. A *"luminous automatic donkey, nodding its head at the end of the upstairs hall."*

What upstairs hall? What was Russell talking about? When we knew him, he was selling old books out of the back of a dusty store on East Tenth Street. I used to go in now and then, and once bought back my husband's grandfather's Gibbon—still with the nameplates. Russell never married, though we heard later there had been a "friend" all along, so at least that. As well as his hideous dog, Rose, whom I knew, in a way, more intimately than I knew Russell, since she had bitten me once.

In my own loft, no less, when we still lived in Little Italy. Russell had walked up the stairs with her, as if she were a regular dog and not a menace to society, and though I was slightly surprised, since he hadn't mentioned a dog, I bent, naturally, to pat the beast just as Russell cried out, "No, don't!"

Too late—my hand was already in Rose's mouth by then.

I'd grown up in the days when dogs ran loose through the neighborhood, even dogs that were rumored to bite, but I'd never been caught by one before. The amazing thing was that as Rose was biting, I looked into her eyes, and she into mine, and something passed between us, and she still bit, but only a little. It was one of those moments people must have had with animals all the time in the old days. A true interchange, almost the original agreement.

And I can still see her, small, black, and snarling, more clearly than I see Russell—I vaguely remember him wearing a cap, Maoist, I think, though that might have been less politics than because things were cheap in Chinatown. And the jacket, again Chinese, though again, all this has been contested by others who knew him better. But they can't tell me what he used to wear either, so it ends up seeming not to matter. And what we do agree on is that there would have been no well-turned profiles from Russell, he wasn't that sort, even if there had been any more grand family photos in those days, which there weren't.

Though of course there should have been, and how could I not have at least gotten out my old Polaroid and snapped a shot? And there were all those photographers around us—some of the Warhol guys who liked to photograph my husband, and the light in the loft was good. And there was that girl in the Village with blue chemicals in her bathtub who could develop anything, even taken at night with no meter, anything—but where are the photos of that night? Of any night?

Snap them, I want to say to my young friends, but I guess they do. Their problem is the opposite one. They are drowning in images, while we are crawling on the shore for even one.

Too bad, but, *"Mine is the outer darkness,"* as Russell wrote in one of his poems.

Russell. Cap or not, Chinese jacket or not, ill-bred phosphorescent mongrel snarling on a leash, living in a slum apartment somewhere in the East Village when it was the East Village, a short flight even for a raven with a broken wing from the grand house on Union Square where both mothers, Molly's and Russell's, along with Uncle Edward and his brothers, had all been born. With a cow in the backyard in those days, the 1880s, and a carriage out front, and silver and crystal, and the upstairs and downstairs they show on all that English TV. And though Russell's familial fortunes seem to have followed the same declivity as Molly's, there was not, in his own case, a lack of education. He was a boy. Someone saw to it.

And in fact, I heard recently that he went not just to Harvard but to Yale as well, "the only one in the family to do so," the last old cousin told me, but he didn't graduate from either. Class of 1947, he should have been. But one of his brothers, a fighter pilot, was shot down in the war with the RAF, fighting Rommel, and then his sister, the person to whom he was closest in this world, was hit by a bus on a Cambridge street.

Most people recovered. Even that kind of loss, double and compounded, didn't stop most of them from finishing college and becoming lawyers or bankers or the local insurance man, and doing perfectly all right. Getting unto themselves the house on the hill, or three bedrooms on Park Avenue, and beating on.

Not Russell, though. *"My dream is a life,"* he wrote in one of his poems, *"in which nothing happens . . . I have had my luck."* And maybe he had, he must have, to write that, though of what that consisted there is no record. He speaks of a *"well-wishing crone"* who gave him a good-luck piece *"in sad green Arcady where I was born."*

He took what was supposed to be a year off from college and went to England, where he lived with a friend of his mother's, and worked, Simone Weil–style, on the assembly line in a roller skate factory. From there he came back not to Cambridge but to New Haven, and finally New York, sans degree, where he lived with an elderly cousin and edited a poetry magazine.

And as to his trajectory from there and all that, to the back corner in what its owner called an antique store, though in another mood she might have had them paint "Junque" on the window—was he gay already? Had he chosen what people were starting to call a downtown lifestyle? Or had it chosen him?

Picked him out as an outcast, a fellow traveler, one of those men who would not in this life stand among the "providers." A man who would do whatever it took, forsake whatever was left of what he'd been born to, to evade the clutches of a fertile woman who would soon be producing her own little Mollys and Fannys and Neds, all of whom would look up at him this time, with hope in their beady little eyes, when he staggered in the doorway every night, his own definitive work also unwritten.

The very thought of that must have made his knees go weak. And whether that led him to the Luxor Baths midtown or the Anvil downtown, or neither, it did lead him to the little shop, and to Rose, and to us. He probably saw us as at least possible, the way the cousins in his own generation were not. We weren't lawyers or bankers, we lived downtown, there were always bad stairs and strange people and who-knew-what in the offing. He once walked into the Broome Street Bar on a quiet afternoon, and caught me in the act of sniffing cocaine right off the bar with a greaser friend of my husband's called Sabu, who introduced himself to Russell as "an American Indian from Brooklyn," and offered him a line.

I was horrified, but Russell seemed unperturbed. He declined politely, but sat down with us and ordered a lemonade.

I'm not sure of that, however. It might have been a triple Stoli.

The books he sold were beautiful, wonderful, and we know where he got his taste, and even most of his stock. One of his rich aunts, sharing Russell's distaste for children, though not his forbearance, for she'd had them, now seemed to take pleasure in dispossessing them. She turned over their father's library to Cousin Russell, and let him disperse it over the Lower East Side.

And I bought back what I could, though mostly in reduced form, because many of the fine old bindings had been ruined in a plumbing event at Russell's apartment, and he'd had them rebound with plain old blue cloth, which looks nice now, compared to the way the new books come out. But at the time seemed tragic.

But, "Never mind," I told myself, an expression I'd picked up from Cousin Betty. And along with the Gibbon, I bought Hawthorne and Kipling and Teddy Roosevelt. Not much competition for those in the seventies, but it was still good of Russell to give me a discount, though I didn't necessarily need it then.

And once I even bought a table from his host, a grand old dame herself, Foreign Service, who had lived all over the world, in high style, but then had retired and come down with that bump, that back-to-reality jolt they all get. It really is too bad about our foreign servants, whom we support in such state abroad, but then kick from the garden at the end, without enough money to live in the manner to which we've accustomed them. I've met a few. The story is always the same, a real scramble at the end. Thank goodness the new crop don't seem to study their forebears' history. If they did, they'd never sign up.

But Russell's boss at least had never married, so had wasted no money on children and education, and thus managed to buy a nice old house for herself, though in a sketchy neighborhood, east of Avenue A, on a "terrifying square," as she put it, where in those days even I rarely ventured. But she kept Old Tom, a big black Lab, to protect her, and rented out floors to other state department types who'd seen worse in Lagos and Saigon, and she had the shop as well, where, as I say, I once bought a very bad table—how bad I didn't fully realize until I got it home.

Not that it wouldn't have been fine with a lamp and a fringed cloth in the far corner of an obscure English country parsonage a hundred years ago, with its curlicue legs and six-sided top. But no one would say that it stood to advantage in the middle of a half-empty room on West Fourth Street.

"What's that doing here?" my husband said when he saw it.

"Nothing," I answered, which was soon to be true, but on the other hand, it meant appearing the next morning with the thing at my back and the Foreign Service at my front. Who in this case had not only already cashed my check and paid the light bill with it, but had also just completed to her satisfaction all the shifting and reconfiguring of the myriad single candlesticks and creamers sans sugar bowls, along with the china dogs with one slightly chipped ear, and yellowing doilies that had previously dwelt upon this convenient catchall, which was briefly my table. Not to mention the standing lamps and bedside tables that had already crept into its place, and I have to say, I was really glad to spot Russell about a block away, with Rose breathing fire and pulling him in my direction for more.

I waved to him as I wrestled the table out of the taxi, and into the shop, and started the pushing, pulling, and repositioning of every "antique" in there, some of them heavy and all of them hanging by a thread. And the truth is I was grateful for the penance, because I admired her, Cecil, the owner—she was smart and funny and tough. She told amazing stories—about how in Cambodia, in the sixties, when she was first posted there, large numbers of country people, displaced by the fighting, had fled to the city, where they seemed to be getting hit by cars in unreasonably high numbers. It even looked as if they were crouching on the corners, and jumping out in front of the speeding cars.

Mass suicide? The liberals among the diplomats were concerned. There was an official inquiry—but it turned out that these folks were simply taking advantage of a new weapon in their eternal struggle against the evil spirits who dogged their every step. The idea was that if they timed it precisely, they could just squeak past the car, leaving the ghosts behind to be hit.

And Cecil told us too about how in Sweden, it was so dark on winter mornings that the only way her house-keeper could get her out of bed was to bring a rich dark cup of coffee and waft it under her nose. Nor, imagining Cecil in that bed—the maid, the *kaffe*, the position she'd earned entitling her to such perquisites—was it much of a stretch to imagine how she must have felt about having to cap her career by purveying bad tables, and not even successfully, to Russell's blithe young cousin.

And as the butt of her barely repressed wrath that morn-ing, I have to say that I was watching the door for Russell's arrival, looking forward to Rose's nasty snarl and growl to lighten things up a bit, but in fact Russell didn't actually come in that morning after all. He must have sussed out the whole affair from afar and changed his trajectory, and who can blame him? Better the root canal that he'd been post-poning, or a visit to the tax people, than a scene between women.

Russell had left his place at that table, walked away from everything ruling-class that he still might have claimed— there were no squash games, no dinner jackets, no crisp lin-ens or lawn parties in his life, so why should he be expected to assume the role of paterfamilias one cold morning on East Tenth Street? Looking back, one can see that it would hardly have been fair.

V

Harvard-Yale, 1904

I KNOW WHAT flowers were on the table that night, because I recently found a bill from a flower shop, stuck in an old journal: daffodils and crocuses, a bouquet of delphiniums, lavender freesia, a sterling-silver rose, and a yellow tulip. This extravagance was perhaps to make up for the complete dereliction of flowers growing outside in the Village in those days. Sheridan Square was nothing but broken glass and needles, the old-time junkies huddled on the broken benches, and anytime a crocus or tulip tried to push through the litter in Washington Square (Uncle Edward bristled at the redundancy of "Washington Square Park"), someone quickly trampled it into the dirt. Didn't even take it home, just broke it and threw it on the sidewalk, which was almost enough to make a person a Republican—ask Giuliani. Or James Q. Wilson and George Kelling, whose "broken window" theory, applied to the flowers, turned out to be right. What sent me from New York in those days was in fact the wanton and uncontrolled destruction of public flowers. It was the crime that said it all to me.

And though I fled rather than move to the right, one could

argue that the buying of daffodils and crocuses for private consumption was in fact the classic Republican solution. Cut the hell out of the public's forest, drill their lands, leave their schools and mill towns in shambles, and then with the money you've made doing all that, buy yourself a corner facing away from the desolation, in the expensive part of Wyoming or New Mexico. Get some nice flowers flown out for yourself.

But as for us that night, they were beautiful, those flowers, and we had learned to cook a bit by then, and I saw a soup referenced, though not what kind. Nor did I bother to note the main course, but it would have been leg of lamb, because that's what we always had when Uncle Edward came to dinner. I don't remember exactly how we served it—attempting little potatoes like Betty's, though I don't think we'd come quite that far, nor have we, to this day.

What I do remember, however, is how Uncle Edward would turn to me afterward every time, and compliment me on my "judicious use of garlic."

This I accepted, though did not deserve, since I wasn't the judicious one in this case, but his grandnephew, though we could never bring ourselves to disabuse Uncle Edward of his concept of the cooking of the lamb. That I, his niece by marriage, was the one flushing over the oven, after a controlled and discreet spell of seasoning with a light and graceful hand.

And the funny thing is that I don't think we ever made it again, once we left New York. We've forgotten how, it has passed out of usage. They didn't have it in Brazil, and didn't eat it in Los Angeles. Even the not-bad French restaurants out there that will whip up mousse of unborn sea slugs if you go in with a movie star go blank if you ask for "*gigot*."

But then and there, it was still standard dinner-party

fare, for parents and so forth, and as for dessert, we probably made what we'd learned when we visited Uncle Edward at his country house in the Berkshires—where we had to suppress gasps at the first sight of him not in his three-piece suit, but his country version, gray flannel trousers and pressed plaid Pendleton shirt, buttoned to the top. Perfectly correct and formal too, in its way, but we had never seen or even imagined him in anything but his suits, so weren't prepared, and had to avoid exchanging a glance at first, lest one of us burst out laughing.

Anyway, his equally correct and very nice daughter-in-law, who served as his hostess up there, sent us out with a bucket to pick blueberries and then taught us, or probably me—which was fine because it was terribly easy—to make the old family dessert, "Sat-Upon Pudding." The recipe called for a flatiron as the proper tool for "sitting" the thing, and frowned upon "cultivated blueberries," although one could try sprinkling them with lemon juice, "if you're in the city and must resort to them."

Which we did, from that day forth, resort to, as well as a big triangular rock, dragged into town on the train from a far beach, that seemed a dead ringer for Uncle Edward's flat iron and worked just as well, if somewhat transgressively, for detailing our pudding. Which was probably what we served for dessert that night.

Or if it was too early for even store-bought blueberries, we might have run across the street for pastries at Lanciani's, the first fancy bakery in the neighborhood, but I don't remember if Uncle Edward liked them. At Giovanni's, we always had strawberries with zabaglione. Another thing I never saw on a menu in L.A.

* * *

When Uncle Edward walked in at eight that night and saw Molly in her dirty clothes with her lank, stringy hair, he neither faltered in his step nor blanched. He simply smiled at her—their smile—and she smiled back at him. If he was shocked at the sight of her, he gave no sign. It occurs to me now that he was no more judging Molly that night than he was judging me. That is, he knew who we were—I was his grandnephew's wife in white, even if it was black that evening, and Molly was his dear niece who'd once been clean in a good linen shirtwaist.

Which was truly something for all of us, a real gift, magic almost. For what, then, were the knocks, the kicks in the teeth that this life offers? Nothing at all, since here was Uncle Edward and here were we all, in from the cold, in even from our poor choices, even those that had set us free out there, just because they simply didn't exist for this moment.

So why should Molly have rushed out and put herself through the thoroughly demoralizing act of buying a dress that might have got her wondering why she had wanted to come in the first place? And why should she have bothered to leave work—her rock, her redemption—early, in order to take the kind of bath that would encompass a shampoo and thus a confrontation with the mirror that had long since been put conclusively aside? Avoided like the plague, and for the same reason. The danger, the potential contagion, from the mirror to her, in through the eye—again, fair enough. So why put herself through any of that, when all she had to do was stumble over just as she was, even at her worst, her very worst, and be received as herself, plain and simple, by Uncle Edward?

"Hullo, Molly"—Uncle Edward kissed her, or shook her hand. Whichever it was that they did. Molly thanked him again for being so nice to her on that train, sixty years ago.

Uncle Edward remembered—said something about her being a very good child, and quite sick that time. Molly was beaming. He turned to Russell—a handshake here, definitely. These men didn't hug. And Russell, who'd leapt to his feet to greet him, looked at the same time solicitous and very young.

What I wish I could remember was how Betty had reacted to the sight of her sister Molly, but the fact that I don't is to her credit. Had she looked askance or said something sotto voce, I would have noticed. Recorded it. I was a close student of life in those days.

So Betty was either accustomed to Molly looking like a Bowery bum, or she was as good a player as Uncle Edward, better actually. Since in her case it would have taken discipline, whereas with Uncle Edward it was more of an absolute. A Zen state, to which this ultra-patrician, uber-WASP New Yorker who had probably never visited so much as the then-negligible Asian wing at the Metropolitan Museum, let alone a Buddhist meditation site, had somehow evolved.

Or maybe it was simpler than that, more personal, familial. Something in the blood that admitted no outward interference. Wouldn't deign to acknowledge the mere vicissitudes of life, that had altered perhaps the outward state of this one or that one. True, they had their family crests and some of the aunts by marriage kept up the charts of their direct descent from Longspee, William the Conqueror's son and the first knight buried in Salisbury Cathedral. But their real motto, I would submit, was something one of them had mentioned in passing at a wedding. "Some of the family are rich and some are poor, but you can never tell which is which."

The flowers that night reminded Uncle Edward, he said, of his great-grandmother. The one who died just short of her hundredth birthday and whom Uncle Edward had known when he was a young boy. And she, as a young girl, had known George Washington. Her father was Roger Sherman, and the then–General Washington had come to their house in New Haven, either about the Declaration of Independence or the new United States, which came into being as a result of the visit.

Uncle Edward's great-grandmother had wanted to see the great man for herself, so when he was leaving, she ran past the maid whose "office" it was to open the door for visitors, and held the door for him herself.

George Washington stopped and smiled at her. "I might wish you a better office, my little maid," he said.

"Yes sir," she'd answered, "to let you in."

Which was the point to Uncle Edward—more her wit than the name dropped. But a Persian friend to whom we told the tale had gasped and said, "My God! That's like someone's grandmother knowing Cyrus the Great!"

He told us later that when he in his turn repeated the story to some fellow Persians, they'd all shaken their heads—"America!" Which was also an element in Uncle Edward's stories—they were family tales, true, but shed light well beyond the circle they depicted. We occasionally asked some friends to join us at Giovanni's, one a writer at *Vanity Fair*, the other now locked away in a madhouse, and they too had sat rapt and charmed, those nights, and made the stories their own, ever after.

I recently called the *Vanity Fair* one to ask about an anecdote he'd once quoted in the magazine. He answered the phone at the first ring.

"I thought you were the bankruptcy lawyer," he said. "How did I ever think I could support myself through writing?"

I took my own comfort from that, along the "misery loves company" lines, and asked him if he remembered a war story that Uncle Edward had told one night—"About MacArthur?" I thought.

"No, not MacArthur, Pershing," he said, "on his Mexican expedition." Uncle Edward and his brother had been part of a National Guard unit from Plainfield, New Jersey, probably something like the First City Troop in Philadelphia of today, whose annual exercises usually end with a duck hunt. But in 1916, this unit, married men from the suburbs, expecting a weekend of war games in the Meadowlands, found themselves dispatched down to the Mexican border under Pershing, in hot pursuit of Pancho Villa. "The Punitive Expedition," as it came to be known; they never caught Villa, and reading about it today, the whole thing rings only too familiar, like a preview of Vietnam, though in miniature. The Americans had the technology—in fact, this adventure marked our first use of trucks and planes in combat.

Not that any of it helped in the wild unmapped Sierra Nevada where Pancho Villa and his "golden ones" hid out.

Nor did the fact that the local populace, not necessarily fans of Villa till the Americans rolled in, were wholly unreliable, even actively deceptive, as far as logistical information went. Nor could you tell who was who. All the Villistas had to do to pass as noncombatants was to take off their bandoliers. Apparently they would pass in and out of the U.S. Army bases regularly, and sit among the soldiers of an evening, watching American cowboy films.

"Having dashed into Mexico with the intention of eating the Mexicans raw," wrote Pershing at the time, *"we turned back at the first repulse and are now sneaking home under cover, like a whipped curr with its tail between its legs."* The only time the Americans actually encountered Villa is remembered not for its successful outcome—Villa escaped into the hills—but as "the last true cavalry charge" in our history. And the only one who did anything definitive down there was the young Lieutenant George Patton, who rode out after the enemy in a Dodge touring car and came back with three dead men strapped to the hood. Though it turned out that they might not have been rebels, but just farmers.

If Uncle Edward was there to see Patton's car that day, he didn't say. In fact, none of us remember hearing about any of the historical details—no opinions about Villa himself, nor the American experience in Mexico. What my friend remembered was Uncle Edward telling about one of his acquaintances who collapsed in the heat and the dust down there, and caused them some trouble, "which is exactly what he did during the Harvard-Yale races in 1904," said Uncle Edward. "Collapsed in our boat, and we had to throw the race."

*   *   *

We probably had champagne after dinner, because I remember Uncle Edward proposing a toast, to his recently born great-granddaughter, named Sarah Paine, after his own great-great-grandmother, who had once given a dinner party in Boston before the Revolution that John Adams had attended. It was King George's birthday that day, and someone had offered a toast.

They all drank—"To the King!"—John Adams among them, but then he rose and proposed his own toast, "To the Devil!"

Some of the men in attendance that night wanted to fight, but Sarah Paine the First had risen to her feet, lifted her glass, and said, "Well, gentlemen, he drank to our king, now let's drink to his!"

We raised our own glasses then, to both Sarah Paines, but I mentioned that I was shocked to hear of Tories in the family. I'd thought it was George Washington and Roger Sherman all the way.

But the Boston branch were "loyalists," as Uncle Edward put it. Some of them even decamped to Canada afterward. To them, the Revolution was a case of simple lawlessness, and our great and ancient heroes nothing more than the rabble. Not that it wasn't a bit of the rabble for John Adams to make a scene like that at a formal dinner in what was presumably a fashionable house in Back Bay Boston, although he must have been plenty put out himself, being called to raise a cup to the Mad King George.

But there was John Adams—young, then, and passionate. He'd always been old in my eyes. Old and Founding-Fatherish, never a scamp to raise his glass with mischief in his eye and wit on his tongue. John Adams—who knew? Besides Uncle Edward.

Which was the point, in the end. Why these stories, though all of them hinging on the family, were somehow not really personal. Maybe it was a matter of distance. Of time, "*intolerant*," as Auden put it, to all but the stories.

That night at dinner, Russell ventured that he remembered something about Haiti, "though I might have dreamt it," he hastened to add with that little smile.

Dreamt it? said Uncle Edward. He didn't know about that, but was he asking about his great-grandfather, Russell's great-great-great? A Bostonian who'd found himself in "Saint-Domingue," as Haiti was then called, at the time of the uprising, when the enslaved people were killing all the whites. This particular ancestor had been returning from Africa, when in mid-crossing, he was distressed to come upon a man called Mousse, whom he could see was dying. Since Mousse was a captive, it was forbidden for the ship's doctor to treat him. So the great-great-grandfather had bought him, "simply to save the fellow's life," said Uncle Edward, and then took him to his own stateroom— permissible, since he owned him—and saw that he was fed and treated. Mousse recovered, and when they landed at Port-au-Prince, Uncle Edward's great-grandfather gave him a little money, and set him free.

That would have been in 1804, when the uprising was no longer led by Toussaint Louverture, whose vision, noble, inclusive, and fair, had died with him in prison in France, where he'd been lured and then betrayed. In his place was a new leader, Jean-Jacques Dessalines, who trusted no white man and wanted no trace of them left on the island. He changed the country's name from Saint-Domingue to

Haiti, a version of the old Arawak name, and led his men out on a rampage to rid the island of the race that had terrorized them.

And then it was Mousse's turn to stretch out the hand of mercy. Amid the brutal massacre of white people taking place all around them, and at serious risk to his own life, he managed to smuggle Uncle Edward's great-grandfather back to the ship in the Port-au-Prince harbor, and once onboard, decided to continue with him back to Boston.

Where Uncle Edward, as a very small child, had known him. Mousse was ancient by then, but he would still upon occasion slip into the children's nursery at night, and teach them the war dances he'd learned as a young man in Africa.

"This was at Number Two Walnut Street, on Beacon Hill," said Uncle Edward, lest one wonder. Doubt.

And the last story he told us that night was about an initiation into the Signet Society, a club at Harvard, of a tall football player named Don Nichols. Nichols was first asked, Uncle Edward told us, to demonstrate how a Roman put on his toga.

"Well, he did that all right," said Uncle Edward as we all leaned in, and then Professor Kittering, a bearded sage who taught Latin at the college, and had been an old friend of Russell's father's, asked what the Roman would say as he put on his toga.

"*Arma virumque cano,*" stammered Nichols. The first line of Virgil. Probably all he could summon.

"That's just what he *would* say!" shouted Kittering.

A silly story, but I remember stealing a glance around the table then. All faces were transformed, beaming in the candlelight. Smiling one smile, all around. No one was rich or poor or fallen or lifted up. No one was out in the cold. Life had done nothing. We were all of us worthy. All of us signers of the Declaration of Independence, all of us senators and secretaries of state, and having Edith Wharton to tea. Laughing with Kittering at the Signet, escaping through the dark Haitian night. Greeting George Washington, sailing the fastest clipper ship on the seas, or at least owning it, and then being born in Florence.

And later, summering in the greenest of the green, called Paradise, since it was, Paradise, in the last of the family places, in mid-Vermont. Being brave enough to swim way out in the pond there on a hot, slow summer day, despite the snapping turtles, maybe even the very day the two great-grandfathers, on an outing of their own, were thrown from their carriage on the small hill beneath the cucumber tree, giant now, and killed, both of them. One from Boston, one from New York. An ultimate coming together of the branches.

I turned then to Uncle Edward, seated between Betty and Molly—tall, thin, well clipped in his three-piece-suit, the picture of American rectitude, but a conjurer of the highest order, it came to me, even without a hat of stars or a sprig of oak, ash, and thorn. Still, he had woven a circle round us thrice, and the claret we were drinking that night was the milk of paradise. Nothing less.

It happens sometimes, maybe it's happened to you. Somewhere, anywhere, probably unpredictable. It's not something you can buy or even go after, but when it happens, if it does, you can take note. "Close your eyes in holy dread."

So to speak, because of course one doesn't. What one

does is sit there, smiling, strangely happy, until someone, for some reason—it's probably part of it; there's probably a term in alchemy for the breaking of the spell—notes the time, how late, and you get up from the table, it has come to an end. You walk out into the New York night with the precious beings who are even then receding before you. You have, anyway, plans for your own life that will take you far away. A new being in that line may even then have begun growing, still unnoted, within you. A new life that will bring those New York nights to what seems, looking back, like an early close.

But that night we were still all there, and we would have put Uncle Edward and Betty into an uptown taxi, and then waved goodbye on West Fourth Street. And maybe after that, we walked Molly and Russell partway home. Having locked the door, but left the dishes. The night was beautiful. We were going out.

o fim

Cleveland
Auto Wrecking

I

IT NEVER SEEMED strange to the White brothers that it was called Cleveland Auto Wrecking, even though it wasn't in Cleveland. But that was because they'd all heard the story, or some version—that their father, age thirteen at the time and illiterate, had gotten off the boat alone at Ellis Island with one English word in his head: "Cleveland." It was around 1900. He had relatives in Cleveland, he had been told, someone presumably from the same dark corner of the world that he himself had fled, in what was either Poland or Ukraine at the time, it was never clear. Not that a border made much difference for people like him, who were not only poor but in danger, on either side of any border they knew. And he must have known by the time he was thirteen that he had nothing to gain there, and had already conjured enough of a sense of self to travel—alone? with someone? an acquaintance? a group?—the nine hundred miles from Eastern Galicia to Hamburg, from where most of the boats that were carrying boys like him in those days left.

His passage to the New World would have been the cheapest, the steerage of the steerage. The highest bunk—they were stacked six up—or the one in the middle, whichever was least desirable, in the hottest or coldest part of the hold, whichever was worse, either closest to the boiler or farthest from whatever fresh air made it down from the decks.

But he was thirteen, so maybe less affected by that hardship, maybe not even aware. Maybe he felt like a boy camping out—was a boy camping out, taking everything as it came as simply the way it was. Even the Statue of Liberty—maybe she'd been simply part of the trip, one and the same with the dry crusts and thin soup that had kept him alive on board ship, neither more nor less. Lady Liberty, lamp aloft, good, fine, but nothing to fall to one's knees for, or sing "Hosanna" with the rest of his shipmates. He wouldn't even have known the words.

But there she was, just as there he was, he had made it, with, in his case, a tag on his clothes that matched him up to a name on the passenger list that the customs man on Ellis Island couldn't pronounce. It started with a W, though, and was short. So "White," wrote the man, on a paper he gave the boy. "A new name for a new life," he is said to have told the boy, but whether customs would have bothered or the boy understood his English is anyone's guess.

It would have been fine with the boy anyway, as this last link to his past was cut. He had left nothing there that he would in his long life regret, or at least mention. Did he still have a mother, or had she already died in childbirth, as so many of the lone young immigrants' mothers had? Been replaced by a stepmother who would have been glad enough to see his back? Or was it his father who had died, leaving a woman who, even if she was his birth mother, had barely looked up for a final farewell from the heavy serge piecework she was sewing, hoping more that her needle didn't break than that this dispensable third or fourth son might live through his voyage. God would protect or would not. But if the needle broke on the overcoat she was sewing, the rest of them would not eat that night.

But in this case, God did protect, first on the trip across the bloodlands of Eastern Europe, and then on the sea, stormy or calm, he never said, and finally that day in Ellis Island. He was small for his age—you need more than the groats in thin broth he'd subsisted on to get tall. Still, they didn't stop him there. He was vaccinated for smallpox along with all the other immigrants, and the New York doctors passed him through—no leprosy, no cholera, no trachoma, the deadly eye disease that stopped so many. There was the series of questions he was asked while still on board, and since he mentioned Cleveland, he was herded into a tender that transferred all those headed west onto a ferry, which delivered them nonstop to the Erie Railroad terminal in Jersey City. Forget New York—these folks were headed to the promised lands. Ohio or beyond, Indiana, Minnesota, and among them, this boy with a new name that he probably couldn't pronounce yet, but must have liked. Sam White. An American name.

Like the names he would have heard but couldn't read as they steamed away from the water—Binghamton, Elmira, Hornell, Jamestown. Maybe it was here that he fell asleep, as the train crawled along the south shore of Lake Erie and the first small towns, their outskirts, their shabbiest houses, even their clotheslines revealing secrets, thrilling mysteries, of his new land. But when they came to the lake itself, he could have closed his eyes—he had seen enough water lately, enough for a lifetime, it turned out. No seaside holidays, no cruises in this boy's future. Not even years later, when he could.

Eventually the Erie Limited turned away from the lake and went south. The railroad had a big immigrant trade in the early years of the twentieth century, and there would have been others in the battered coaches where Sam White found himself. Someone who would have spoken his language, but probably not English, so when they heard the conductor calling out, "Ohio," maybe they thought Ohio was Cleveland, and woke the sleeping boy. Helped him off, kindly, at the wrong stop.

In Youngstown, not Cleveland—not an uncommon way for fate to apportion lifetimes to these young immigrants in those days, 1902, 1903. Why he didn't take the next train on to Cleveland some time later, no one ever thought to ask. Anyway, that card laid where it was played, as he could say in German and Russian but not yet in English, and Sam White stayed where he had landed. Though years later, in an uncharacteristic nod to earlier dreams, he named his wrecking yard "Cleveland," after that near miss.

The future. Between that substantial business and the bewildered search for Cleveland in Youngstown lay fifty years. One can pretty much get that personal story from the overall one—Youngstown was a growing steel hub then, halfway between both Cleveland and Pittsburgh, and New York and Chicago, which seemed to mark out a special destiny for the town. Helped along by that tide that in the first half of the twentieth century eventually lifted all boats, including Sam White's.

But what about his first night? Aged thirteen with no

English? There were said to be men who met those trains, seeking the same kind of desperate cheap immigrant labor that we see these days on certain street corners in Santa Monica, and maybe one of them gave Sam White a place to sleep and a shovel. Meals with people who spoke his language.

Not that there would have been much in the way of conversation around a table like that. These weren't the gregarious Hungarians, arriving with a book or two in their leather cases, who would later open the pharmacies and the good men's clothing stores, and send their own sons to college and med school. Nor were they the Poles, who already had their churches and kielbasa suppers on Sundays, and got the jobs opening up at the mills. Sam White wouldn't have had a seat at those suppers. He came from a more downtrodden people, people who didn't teach their children how to read, not the kind with a helpful hand to hold out, on this side of the Atlantic either. The only mention his sons ever heard about a relative featured a brother or half brother, older, with whom Sam White worked somewhere for a while. This brother had cheated him on some kind of deal, and they'd argued. As the young Sam White was stomping out, his brother hurled a brick at him, and caught him in the back. Knocked him unconscious and left him for dead.

But someone dragged him to a hospital, and he lived, recovered, though didn't press charges. America was a foreign country, and who knew what might come from tangling with the law here? Where he came from the law was a threat, a violence to be avoided, even fled. Or maybe it was more that the crime of fratricide at least had some history, some context, unlike so much else in his young life then, ringing an old bell he hadn't heard since he crossed the gray sea. Calling back the only stories he remembered from his mother's lips, or maybe his father's. Cain and Abel. "I am not my brother's keeper."

But whatever it was, he took it for a warning, and moved on alone. His own sons grew up knowing nothing of that brother. Three sons Sam White eventually had—whom he named, improbably, Royal, Melvin, and Bertram. Or maybe it was his wife who'd come up with the names. She too had come over from the same God-knows-where as Sam White, she too was poor and illiterate, though with a twinkle in her eye that never went out. How she'd landed in that same corner of northeastern Ohio, how they ever met, let alone married, is shrouded in the same mists as so many of these stories.

But through another lens, not personal but demographic, it made perfect sense. Youngstown was attracting the world in those days. There were steel mills, growing, expanding, everything was expanding there around the turn of the century. This was a part of the world that a hundred years earlier had been inhabited successfully by people who shot duck, caught fish, gathered chestnuts and berries, and mostly left the place alone. These Eastern Europeans who'd grown up scratching up groats and barley on overgrazed steppes were awed by what they'd arrived to—the greenest land, tallest trees, rivers, and work for everyone, including peddlers, which was the best Sam White could do at first. With a cart, and eventually what must have been an old horse, he went through the streets, collecting first anything, old paper, rags, and then narrowing it down to metal. "Scrap."

Which was enough, then, with some radical economizing—a boiled egg for lunch. Secondhand clothes, shoes, no such thing as Saturday night or even Sunday—to get married and even support a family. Enough, by the late 1920s, to buy a house, which he lost to the banks in the Depression. Even America couldn't stop that.

The family decamped to a decrepit rental in the poorest part of town, next door to another family called White, who were, however, Black. They'd found themselves in similar straits as their white counterparts due to the fact that the Black people who'd come up from the South to work in the mills found that the essentially Polish unions had closed ranks against them. Blacks were excluded from the steel workers union until 1974, and by then it didn't matter anymore, because most of the mills were closing.

But in the 1930s and especially in the '40s, when things picked up again and union men in Youngstown were earning real living wages—enough to support whole families, mothers-in-law and maiden aunts included—as far as Black Americans were concerned, they kept it, in Bob Dylan's words, "all hid." From Sam White too—he'd only owed a little bit on his house when the bank started nailing notices and then finally sent the sheriff. Sam White wasn't entirely surprised at that piece—the law serving power. But as for rising with tears in his eyes for "The Star Spangled Banner" like so many of his counterparts—the Poles, the Hungarians—Sam White was never quite there after that.

So he left his piece of the American dream to the Mahoning National, and moved to the ragged part of town with the other excludeds, only he managed to pull himself together again in a way that they never did. Because, though he never learned to read, for some reason he could work with numbers—not written, but in his head. One can only wonder what early training in a broken-down village in a war-torn corner would have prepared this negligible boy to be a whiz at figures that he couldn't even read. Maybe it was the very fact that he couldn't read that left room in his mind for the concept of numbers. Maybe it was that, unlike his counterparts, the Black Whites, he had no friends, no church, no Sunday barbecues. What he had instead were his numbers—his barbecues, his friends and relations. All there safe, untouchable, in his head, where no one could take a house or throw a brick.

He didn't talk much to his neighbors or smile, but they didn't take it wrong, because they could see that he didn't talk to anyone, or ever smile, not even at his boys, who were twelve, ten, and eight then, just kids, and went to school with their own children. But after school, those boys went straight to work at the junkyard where Sam White was working then. Every day but Sunday, when it was closed by law.

But on Sunday, he had them at other jobs, even the eight-year-old. This boy was shy, didn't talk much or play in the street, even when his old man was out and he could have. The one they liked best though, the Black Whites, was the oldest one, Roy. He was out all the time, taking marbles off their boys, smiling at their girls, and they even taught him to dance, and he was pretty good, had all the moves, with that big smile of his that seemed collusive somehow. Seemed to bring them all in on whatever mischief he had up his sleeve.

The little one, called B., didn't smile much, except the time his old man came home with a bicycle for him. Old, used, repainted a dull black, but a bike. Beautiful. It wasn't even Christmas—not that Christmas meant much in either of those White houses, not in the thirties. No one had the money. Sometimes just enough for a ham for the Black Whites, but sometimes not.

But that bike—it must have been summer, because the little kid, B., was out on that bike right away, wobbling in the street, learning to ride. Then riding, and laughing in a way they'd never seen, with pure joy, up and down the street, eyes front, but laughing, filled with that bike, the delight of it all. Life on a summer evening—they caught it too, sitting on their porch. They were all poor, tenants all, but all of them on that bike too, that night.

But then the old man—not so much old as heartless, truly heartless, the neighbor Whites concluded then—took the bike back because the kid forgot his chores one time. Just once, jumped on the bike instead of sorting screws or whatever it was, and that was it. Sam White, not even looking at the kid, picked up the bike, and walked off with it. No second chances. It was gone, taken away. Never coming back. Sold for scrap. Whatever.

And that little boy B. didn't cry, but stood in the street looking after his old man long after he was gone, in disbelief, or maybe not. He must have known his father by then. So maybe it was more heartbreak, and Mrs. White, the Black one, sent one of her own kids out to get him out of the street and bring him up on their porch for some of her peanut brittle. And then one of the younger girls took him to the side and taught him to jump rope, and later, to dance. And he took to them both, like he'd taken to the bike, with the same smile on his face, and he turned out to be the best of them all.

II

He wasn't voted best dancer, though, in his high school class. That slot belonged to the Black kids. Nor did he get one of the white slots, like "Most Likely to Succeed." That went to one of the Jewish boys, who were headed to college to become CPAs. B. neither went or even dreamed of going to college. His parents thought it coddling enough, American-style, to let their boys finish high school. And in B.'s case, since he graduated from high school in 1942, with World War II raging, he took the same route of most of his classmates and followed them into the Army.

For some reason—bad lungs, flat feet—he was assigned to the Seabees and sent to the South Pacific, where he built airstrips in the jungles, roads through the strangling vines, confronted fifty kinds of dysentery and even elephantiasis, often under fire, but like so many of them, never talked about any of it afterward. The only mention he ever made of his war years was to observe, once, that he'd been slated to land in Japan ahead of the invading U.S. forces, and was expecting to be killed, they all were, every man in his company, along with more than half of the paratroopers and whoever else was to be involved in that push. Until the atom bomb saved their lives.

Because that was that over there, and although B. was part of what amounted to the post-bomb invasion of Japan, it was no longer under fire. He came home with a few small vases that his mother kept for years, and some pictures of himself with his buddies, all in uniform, on a Japanese street. He's smiling, they're all smiling, they're Americans, they had won the war, and they were coming home to the most sustained boom in American history.

The father, Sam White, too old to be drafted, had stayed behind, and as the country pulled itself out of the Depression, he did too—thanks in both cases to the war. Goodyear Aircraft in Akron was making planes at full capacity, and Willys-Overland in Toledo was turning out what would eventually be 330,000 jeeps for the Army. Suddenly scrap metal was at a premium. Towns were melting down Civil War cannons, housewives turning in pots and pans, and farmers filling trucks with old farm tools and tractors, but the factories still needed everything Sam White could get his hands on, as well as all that the Youngstown steel mills could pump out.

The skies over the city turned orange and gray-blue from the sulfur and coal tars released to fuel the process, but to Sam White, those were the colors of prosperity. "Good for the country," he told his wife. The Mahoning River no longer froze in the winters, no matter how cold it got, due to the red-hot slag the mills were pouring straight into it. "Good for the country," he said to his boys.

America. Which had worked out for him after all. Once

he'd figured it out—that if you're selling something they want, they will buy it, as simple as that. No restricted lists, no baptismal certificates required. No walls to keep you in or out, no lines you couldn't cross, as long as what you were hauling across was unstressed steel that could be made into munitions.

In fact, as the war went on, Sam White slowly put together enough money to buy a small piece of empty land on the south side of town, near where he and the other Whites lived, to use as storage, and, eventually, a proper junkyard. "An eyesore," claimed Esther Hamilton, the local busybody columnist, who wanted him to "beautify" his chain-link fence, but to Sam White, it was beautiful already.

Confirmation that he'd been right after all, to push his way across the sea, despite the setbacks along the way. The brick in the back. The futile struggle to keep his house. The helplessness that sometimes almost overwhelmed him in those early days, sent him underwater, night after night, struggling for breath, in dreams where he couldn't swim. Never made it up to the surface. He would wake, panting, in a cold sweat, once, twice, every night. He had two old shirts he slept in. A good night was when one had dried by the time he'd soaked through the other. Those nights he found himself wondering which turn had been the wrong one, all the way back to the day at age thirteen, when he stepped onto the boat to New York.

But life in America carried people along in the forties, and it turned out he didn't need a brother, and soon found himself prepared to pay cash for another house, a better one, on the North Side this time. One could even say that his American debt—whatever the country owed him for risking it all, crossing the sea for it, for dreaming of the

America for which his sons were then fighting—was now settled. He had given all. He had gotten all. "Fair exchange is no robbery," as one of the women in the boardinghouse where he'd first landed, all those years back, used to say, in English, as she double-jumped him in checkers and took his penny.

It was just before he moved away from his neighbors, the Whites, that they got wind of a rumor—Sam White had a girlfriend on the side. There were nights when his '36 Chevy Standard was neither seen nor heard chugging up Poland Avenue, and the small smile they caught now and then stealing across his face couldn't necessarily be attributed to his junkyard. It was almost a replica in miniature of the smile that they knew from his oldest son, that bad boy Roy, whom they always kept an eye on when their girls were around. An attractive smile, one that might draw in someone who hadn't seen it before. A promise of fun, but as the Black Mrs. White knew, nothing guaranteed beyond that.

"Come into the house, Claudine," she'd call to her older daughter when Roy White came around with that smile, and the girl's reluctance to come only confirmed her suspicions. She baked a cake for them when the white Mrs. White came by to tell her they were leaving, but she wasn't entirely sorry to see them go. Her girls were, though, and so were her boys. In fact, one of them had started working at their junkyard full-time during the war. He left school for it, but that was all right: Since Black men were excluded from the unions, and thus work at the mills, this was as good a start as he would get, diploma or no diploma.

The war ended, and all three of Sam White's sons came home and went to work at the junkyard, their wages rolled back into the family business. A few years later, a big parcel of empty land outside of town came up for sale. Ten acres or so, and Sam White surprised the world and bought it. When he went to the bank or the lawyers or whoever it was that closed the deal, he arrived without a scrap of paper. He had the numbers in his head. No literature, poetry, or even the newspaper headlines to get in the way of whatever numbers went into this or any transaction. He took Roy along to read any fine print.

And once he'd bought that land, he had his own boys, along with some of the Black Whites, move his scrap metal on a flatbed truck across town. After they'd unloaded at the new place, Sam White took a look around, and told his sons that the wasteland around them was now an auto wrecking yard.

No one could call these sons of his dreamers, but they too were riding the rising tide. There were a few old car wrecks among the junk from the other yard. Once they had these pulled apart, they could offer not only scrap metal, but salvaged car parts. Before long, they got someone to tack together a plywood office and someone else to paint a sign.

"What are you calling it?" the painter asked. The sons turned to their father.

"Cleveland Auto Wrecking," he said.

It was around then that the two older boys got married, Roy to someone from Cleveland, and Mel to a woman from Girard, a small tough town nearby. They'd all been living together in the new house that Sam White had bought, and Roy and Mel stayed on, wives notwithstanding, the rent-free aspect eclipsing all the good reasons against such a step. The women hated each other, but neither wanted to leave the field to the enemy. Roy's wife was the first to produce a baby—a girl who didn't look like him, especially if you did the math. Which, being people of the ledger, the Whites did, but being, as well, folk of few words, didn't mention. Figured Roy could take that as he would. As for the rest of them, they loved the child. Didn't require a blood test for that.

Then Mel's wife followed suit with a boy, but anyone coming by of an evening would find the one giving that baby his bottle was Mel. They hadn't quite put together that the "sick mother" Mel's wife was always visiting was in fact a local hoodlum, until one night a bullet came whizzing through an upstairs bedroom window facing the street. It happened to be where Roy's baby girl was sleeping, and the next day, he and his wife left for Cleveland. Her father had some kind of business going on up there, although Roy didn't say what. Just that it wasn't scrap metal. He wouldn't be competing.

"You can call it Youngstown Auto Wrecking if you do," his mother teased him. As for her, it was around then that she announced that she'd had enough of "me being married, when he isn't," as she put it to her sons one evening, indicating Sam White's empty chair. She had a cousin in California, and was going out for an extended visit. Sam White could come or not.

And he might not have, if she'd gone to the cousin in Baltimore, or the one in New York. But west had always been where his luck lay, and as he loaded up the two-tone

Buick that he'd bought, secondhand this time, up from
third, he lifted his head for a moment and felt young again.
Younger even than he had with the girlfriend. The promise of a new beginning trumped even that in his soul. He
hadn't known it till he saw the road map his sons had laid
out on the kitchen table, the thick red lines. The new inter-
states, Eisenhower's work. Sam White had voted for Adlai
Stevenson, but still "liked Ike," especially as he leaned over
that map.

"You want me?" he asked his wife, not that it mattered.
He was going.

"Do I have a choice?" she asked the room in general, but
with her twinkle.

B. was delegated to drive them out, since he was the one
who wasn't married. Maybe he'd find someone for himself
out there and stay, his mother told Roy. At least that's what
she was hoping.

But he didn't, he came back to Cleveland Auto Wrecking and moved back into the house with the bullet hole
in the front bedroom window. Mel's wife had left by then,
but her tough-guy boyfriend was making some noise about
getting more support money from Mel. There had been a
few threats. One of the junkyard dogs the White brothers
let loose at night to roam the perimeter had bitten a guy
who clearly wasn't there to steal hubcaps. They found some
spare bullets that must have fallen out of his pocket near
the fence he'd jumped to get away from the dogs, which
for some reason he hadn't shot, despite the fact that they'd
ripped one of the legs off his cheap shiny pants.

B. gave the dogs a bone and went downtown to eat some

veal scaloppine at Cicero's Restaurant. Youngstown was a Mafia town, and he'd gotten Roy's father-in-law, who had some connections, to put in a call to Vince DeNiro. The White brothers were small fry who just wanted to be left alone with their wrecking yard, the father-in-law explained to DeNiro. And they might even come in handy in the future. "You never know when you can use a wrecking yard," the father-in-law had pointed out.

Which DeNiro must have figured was true, not to mention the fact that Mel's ex-wife's boyfriend had gone back to his wife. The guy was a hothead anyway, and no one's brother or son, so there wouldn't be any more bullets through the White brothers' windows, or any further visits to the yard at night, DeNiro assured B. over the veal. He called for some zabaglione, pulled out a cigar—"what JFK smokes, right off the plane from Cuba"—and made the check go away. B. pocketed the cigar and told DeNiro to come by if he ever needed any parts for his car.

"Cadillacs don't need parts." Vince smiled at B.

"True." B. smiled back, showing the gap between his front teeth for the first time that night, a real smile. "But when they do, we've got 'em. Don't forget."

And maybe Vince did or maybe he didn't, but it turned out not to matter either way. There had recently been one of those gangland power plays going on around town, and Vince had won. His main rival, Sandy Naples, had been gunned down, along with his Polish girlfriend—poor kid, but "wrong place, wrong time," went the general shrug. And then when the next Naples brother, Billy, tried to move in on a piece of the numbers games, he was blown up in his car. The consensus was that Vince was behind both jobs, and the police had him in for questioning, but as usual there were no witnesses. They had to watch him drive off in his Cadillac, top down, *the undisputed kingpin in the Youngstown rackets*," as the Youngstown *Vindicator* put it.

Although a few weeks later, around midnight, as Vince DeNiro stepped out of Cicero's and slipped into the Cadillac, lit one of his Cubans, and turned on the ignition, it was his turn. He too was blown to high heaven, in an explosion so intense it shattered windows and shook houses "*for twenty blocks around*," according to the paper.

The police combed what was left of the car for evidence, but all they found was the same nothing—no evidence, no witnesses—they'd found in the Billy Naples car bombing. Whoever Vince had paid to do away with Naples had probably done this job as well, and the police lieutenant said he wished he could call Vince DeNiro back for a few minutes, just to point this out to him, watch it land, and then maybe get a few names.

But the ones they did call were the White brothers, to come and tow the wreck away, so the Cadillac ended up at Cleveland Auto Wrecking after all. B. and his brothers shook their heads—they'd liked Vince. Then B. remembered the cigar, which he found when he went home that night, still in the pocket of the suit he'd worn to Cicero's. An Upmann, "what JFK smokes," he told his brothers. Leave it to Vince, they all agreed. B. went out on the porch, lit it. The best cigar he ever smoked.

III

Once the elder Whites moved west, B. had planned to get a place of his own, but he ended up staying put, with Mel. The house was there, set up, he had his room, and it was close to the yard. And nice, the nicest place they'd ever lived, on a street that marked the edge of town, and the county as well. Gypsy Lane it was called, and in the old days, that had been true, carny types would come and camp there late in the summer, and set up a little fair with booths and plenty of pickpocketing for all. They'd been replaced by a municipal golf course, but the rest of that county was still semi-rural, to the point that its denizens refused to change their clocks when daylight saving came around.

"The cows don't hold with daylight saving, and neither do we," the farmers told the county commissioner, whose own cows didn't hold with it either. Which meant that for a while, until the farmers got replaced by the city dwellers spilling into the new split-levels that started popping up, Cleveland Auto Wrecking was officially on cow time. Not that it mattered to the White brothers. They rolled in with the sun anyway, and left around the time the cows came home. When business was over.

Mel had recently gotten remarried, and rather than moving out, he had his new wife move in. She liked his brothers, especially B., the quiet one, who seemed to appreciate her cooking and was almost always around for a game of gin of an evening. Roy was there only when he and his wife were fighting, which was often enough that he kept his own bedroom. Never said whether he'd be there for supper or not, just showed or didn't, as if it were still his parents' house and he was the golden boy.

Mel's new wife, Rhonda, didn't seem to mind. There were a lot of laughs when Roy was around; at least, she found herself laughing. Shaking her head and laughing, though Mel didn't find him so funny, and B. too would try not to laugh as Roy made his jokes, cigar in mouth, about their customers, their wives, his wife, his girlfriends. But Roy was funny, and B. would eventually laugh, even as he picked up the pieces from Roy's mistakes—the divorce that finally came to pass, and the settlement that somehow Cleveland Auto Wrecking ended up paying, in one fell swoop, to make sure it went away. Since they remembered that Roy's ex-wife's father was the one who'd put in the call to the Youngstown Mafia when they'd needed it, and who did they have to put in a call to him?

No one, so they paid out of the business, which meant Mel and B. too were paying for Roy's mistakes, which he took for granted, no questions asked. No explanations offered either, or even thanks. This went without saying, as it always had, though there was a moment when B. turned to Mel, and said, "This okay?"

But Mel didn't answer, since it was less a question than an

acknowledgment, public, between them, of Roy's duplicity, and further than that they were not prepared to go. Especially since the money was there, and they were neither of them ready to tear the business apart or go it without Roy— so they paid. Business was good, and Mel's wife had him pull the naked women off the walls in the wrecking yard office, so she could start coming in a few days a week to do the books. They hadn't needed this when Sam White was around—he did the books in his head, and the few times they'd had to turn to an accountant, the guy had been astounded at the way the old man had it to the penny. And though they were all good at figures, they weren't good like their father, who seemed to have a decimal system always running inside his head.

But since Sam White had never learned to read, how did he represent numbers? Could he read them, see them? One day, after looking over some ledgers from their father's bank accounts, Roy had looked up and said, "How do you think he does it? What does he see in his head?"

B. hadn't understood what he was getting at, but Mel's wife Rhonda said she'd wondered too and asked him.

The three brothers turned to her with one look of astonishment across all three faces. That she'd thought to ask, dared to ask. That she'd been so daring and/or foolish as to ask Sam White a personal question, about money, no less—no one did that. Years ago, he'd whipped Roy, badly, with his belt, for asking why the bank had pinned a notice to their door.

"What did he say?" they asked her.

She laughed. "He said he saw it all in terms of '*Gerstengarben*,' something like that. 'From the old country,' he said. I think he meant haystacks."

"Barley bundles," said the three brothers, together.

Of course, it couldn't be true, could it? Their father putting together a life for himself and for them all in a foreign land, counting it all up in bundles of barley? All the barley in America wouldn't pay for Cleveland Auto Wrecking, but the cold hard cash that Sam White must have somehow been translating into some version of barley bundles did— or was he joking? Teasing his new daughter-in-law, with her nice pearl earrings, something they'd never seen before in that family? Something that might have intimidated Sam White a bit, unless he had his little laugh with her.

Or maybe he meant it—that it had started with the barley, something he knew, until he could tie it to something else in his mind's eye, like bundles of dollar bills, and then twenties. Hundreds now. Their mother had called long-distance on Sunday to say that their father had started buying land out in the desert. "Rubble," she said, "like the face of the moon. Good money for that!" She said she thought he'd gone crazy.

"It's a wasteland," she said. "No water, no trees—"

"There are trees," Sam White called out from the background.

"Cactus!" said Mrs. White. "Worse. Strange, ugly—"

"Joshua trees," shouted her husband. "Like from the Bible."

"The desert, where people were left to wander for forty years!" She thought one of the boys should come out to stop him, or at least have a look. She missed the grass, she said, missed the elm trees that lined the streets of Youngstown. "The *ulms*," she said. They'd had elm trees wherever it was that she'd been born, and they'd struck a chord in the strange land where she was sojourning her life away.

But the *ulms* in Youngstown were dying, her sons told her. The city was chopping them down and planting maples, and some kind of pines.

"Spruce," said Rhonda.

"Tiny, saplings, nothing," said Roy. He told his mother she was better off there.

The other boys nodded. She didn't ask to speak to them. Long-distance was expensive, and it was a given that Roy, her first, her favorite, would talk for them all. And what he was saying was that despite their mother's concern, if Sam White was trading barley bundles for land in the California desert, it might not be such a bad thing in the end.

"What town is it near?" Roy asked her.

"Palm Springs," they could hear their father shouting in the background.

As for them in Youngstown, business was—they would never say booming. They too had suffered the forfeiture of their house in the Depression. The possibility of great and cataclysmic loss was always lurking. But there was no denying that business was good, strong, they were growing. It was 1963. They were coming to be the first place in the tri-county region that people came in order to replace their fenders or bumpers or whatever else they needed, in those days before easy money and car leasing. When people still bought their cars outright, and had to keep them going as long as they could.

They were also making a name for themselves as providers not just of old bumpers, but a certain reliable expertise as well, like the kind of good restaurant where the owner is always on the spot. Mel had the whole yard memorized, Sam White–style. He knew every fender, bumper, car door, year, and make that they had on the premises any given day, as well as where it was on the ten-acre expanse. And they had the kind of team too, whose lives, like theirs, were Cleveland Auto Wrecking.

Their old neighbor, Ben White, had become their dedicated wrecker driver. They'd get a call, from as far away as Campbell, south of town, or even Sharon, Pennsylvania, and he'd get on the phone, assess the situation, and take out their tow truck or flatbed, depending, and bring in whatever wreck it was. B. would then come out and have a look, and then call over Matt, the mechanic-in-chief, who would give each metal part either a thumbs-up or thumbs-down. He was never wrong. In the early days of his employment, they occasionally asked him to work on a part he'd rejected, and he never argued, he'd just shrug and have a go, wasting both his time and their money, and after a few of these, the White brothers stopped questioning him. "He's an artist," proclaimed the girl, Sheri, who helped Rhonda in the office, and then the guys in the yard started calling him "Picasso."

He didn't look up at this or anything—he never spoke or smiled, except on payday, when he'd take his check, the minute he got it, to Ace Cash, and then stop in at Al's long enough to get completely blitzed. Then he'd drive very slowly back with his bimonthly smile on his face, and squat down in his little workplace for however long it took for him to finish his work for that day.

"Hey, why don't you take the rest of the day off?" B. would sometimes offer, but Picasso never even looked up to answer.

"When you goin' to Tod's?" was the most you could ever get from him. Tod's being the dive across the road, where the White brothers bought steak sandwiches on toast with big red beefsteak tomatoes for the crew every day, both the regulars and the local derelicts who would cycle through when sober enough for heavy lifting, or to set fire to the worst of the wrecks.

College boys too, home for the summer—there was plenty of work for the unskilled around the place. Endless tires to be lined up, sorted by size, and then hefted up onto specially built racks. Refurbished parts to be delivered to car dealers and body shops around town. Transmissions to be taken out to Old Man Paul—B. was once writing him a check, and asked him if Paul was his first name or last name. There was a long pause, and Old Man Paul, rather than answering, asked B. if he didn't have cash instead. B. told Mel afterward he thought maybe the guy didn't remember.

"His own name," B. said. He'd been "Old Man Paul" that long.

He lived alone, in one of those tiny wood frame houses that used to dot the countryside around there, painted pink or yellow, signifying, maybe, an optimistic lightheartedness back when they were built, postwar. But what they'd come to mean by then was just plain failure. Loneliness. Desolation. The possibility of a turn to bad religion, or even nudist camps, rumor had it, down in West Virginia. Some attempt to catch the tail of that pink or yellow dream, out where what had been country had turned to the sticks.

Old Man Paul wouldn't come into the yard. You had to bring the transmissions to him, up a dirt road, and then a long pitted driveway, slick with mud after rain, choked with dust in the summer, chains required in winter, but on the other hand, no one could fix transmissions like he could. They'd send over the college boys when they had any—they seemed to get a kick out of him. One of them told B. that he'd taken his own rickety Alfa Romeo sports car up that driveway after work, and Old Man Paul fell in love with the transmission. Told the kid he'd buy the car for the transmission, at the end of summer when he went back to school.

But before that could happen, the Alfa was dragged in behind the tow truck that Ben White took out for manageable wrecks. The college boy had a few stitches, but Picasso gave the car a thumbs-down. So they gave the transmission to Old Man Paul—"Christmas in July," said Mel—and had some of the derelicts haul the rest of it over the ridge and burn it.

Which meant dousing the whole thing in gasoline and setting it on fire, a questionable and dangerous practice on any level, but there were few safety or environmental rules operational in that place in those days, and what there were—well, that's why the White brothers were dues-paying Masons. Elks. Sustaining supporters of the Policemen's Benevolent Association. Why they presented themselves, year in, year out, little pins in their lapels, to sit through the chicken à la king and tributes to bad cops and crooked judges at the VFW hall downtown.

"Oh yeah, the White brothers," those cops and judges would say. "I hear you boys are doing pretty well."

"Oh, gettin' by," Mel would concede, and any of them who were paying attention would remember, come "charity" time, to hitch the request up a notch.

IV

MEANWHILE, NOW THAT Roy was divorced, he lived with them permanently. The house was big enough, and Mel's wife Rhonda ran it nicely for them all. She hired one of the Black Mrs. White's friends to live in and paid her the same thirty dollars a week that everyone else got in that neighborhood. At night, they'd generally sit around the card table, except when Mel had his gin club in. On gin club nights, the housekeeper, Willie Mae, would slice the salami and rye bread that was served, without variation, along with Eskimo pies for dessert. Black coffee. They didn't have decaf in those days, and no one in that crowd would have asked for Sanka anyway. They weren't old men.

As for Rhonda, those were the nights when B. took her out to dinner. Cicero's had closed, but there was the Colonial House or the Mural Room, where they'd order their scotch and sodas and veal marsala, or occasionally, the Ding Ho across town, for chop suey. No drinks there, so they'd stop at a bar afterward. They liked each other, Mel's wife and B. He was the kid brother she'd never had. She was the gal he could take out and not have to talk to. Neither of them was sorry that Roy hardly ever came along.

The few times he did, B. would clam up—a different kind of silence from the comfortable one that pertained between him and Rhonda. Not that it was ever remarked upon or even noticed—Roy was accustomed to doing all the talking. He would start by ordering a round of Tom Collinses, his latest drink, without it crossing his mind that anyone might want anything else. And in a way, he was right—who would turn down a good Tom Collins? Once it came and stood there right in front of you, with the little cherry on top.

Though the truth was that gin gave Rhonda a headache, and B. was never really one for sweet drinks. But neither of them said a word—not even a look, unless Roy was distracted, chatting up a waitress with his smile. Then Rhonda and B. would roll their eyes and shrug, while Roy would proceed to order shrimp cocktails—who doesn't like shrimp cocktails? Except B., who was slightly allergic—and steaks, "Sure, fine"—and Thousand Island on the salad, before Rhonda could ask for vinaigrette.

Not that she couldn't have had a side conversation with the waitress, just that she didn't. Neither did B., they just went along and ate what they wouldn't have ordered if Roy hadn't been there.

And then came time for dessert—"What've you got?" Roy asked the waitress.

"Bread pudding," she said.

"My favorite," he'd lie, no matter what it was, and order it for all three.

There was a sign above his desk at the yard: EVERYTHING I LIKE IS EITHER ILLEGAL, IMMORAL, OR FATTENING. Rhonda took it as a joke at first, but had come to see it as narrative. Now, when the stingers came, "on the house"—the owner, sitting in the corner, his back to the wall, lifted his glass to Roy—she figured that they'd hit all three that night. Whatever business Roy had with this guy was definitely not on the books. Illegal most likely, immoral no matter how you looked at it, since he was also cutting out his brothers, and as for the fattening, she and B. lifted the sticky sweet drinks, filled to the brim, crème de menthe running down the sides.

Which they were left to drink alone, since Roy glanced at his watch and got up from the table. It was eight-fifteen.

"Got a date." He winked at Rhonda.

They knew with whom—a beautiful woman from the North Side, whose husband had left her with three children and a big house. She was divorced now, but still reeling. "I'm the only divorced person I know," she'd apparently told Roy when he first asked her out.

He didn't mention his own divorce. He understood that his ilk didn't count. She was from a different world—or used to be. She'd grown up in the better part of town, gone to the better schools. He vaguely remembered that B. had once washed their father's car and driven to the North Side to invite her to a dance, back in high school. But she'd turned him down, with some excuse that wasn't believable even then, to a teenager.

But now the game had changed. Her fancy doctor husband had run off with a nurse, and her parents had had to move into the big house, to pay the bills. Rather than golf games at the country club, she was now enrolled in the local college, scrambling up a teaching degree. Her old friends, girls she'd grown up with, gone to school with, had stopped inviting her to their dinner parties. They couldn't imagine seven at the table. Nine.

And the game had changed for the White brothers too. They lived on the North Side now. The first time Roy approached her, it was in the gas station. He'd pulled his Cadillac up next to her old Buick. A convertible, though. He'd given her credit for that.

He asked her to dinner, but she said she had to put her children to bed. "How about a drink then, afterwards? Eight-fifteen?"

He watched her hesitate, then meet his eyes. She was wary. She looked tired. It hadn't been good. She had loved the bastard.

He smiled. He thought he had her—what did she have to lose now? "One drink, we'll go nearby. You'll be home by nine." She hesitated.

"Okay, ten," he said. She smiled.

That became the drill. She'd have her early dinner with her parents and children, at six or so, when nice families ate then, and Roy would pick her up around eight-thirty. B. always knew when he was taking her out. He'd put on a coat and tie, and smile to Rhonda—"How do I look?" Rhonda never answered. She wasn't a fan of this woman—Jeanette, but Roy, half-teasing, called her "Ned."

The first time Roy brought her over—a Saturday night, when her children had sleep-overs—B. had frozen stiff when she walked in the door. The three of them, Rhonda, Mel, and B., were watching *Gunsmoke*, which was still playing on Saturdays then.

"You know Ned, right?" said Roy. "Rhonda, Mel, B."

"Yeah, sure," said Mel, though no one made a move. They all said hello, but only Rhonda got up. B. kept his eyes on Marshall Dillon.

Ned took it in. "The children love *Gunsmoke*," she said, with a belated, "Me too." But the truth was out—they were subpar.

"Then why the hell is she going out with Roy?" said Rhonda, incensed, to Mel, after she and Roy left for dinner. Which they did as soon as they could muster it. Roy had forgotten something upstairs. B. was half-sick at the thought that it might be a rubber.

It didn't seem fair, didn't seem right to B. He was the one who'd spotted this girl—woman, now—he was the one who'd asked her out twenty years ago, when they were both seventeen. And she wouldn't go out with one of the White brothers then, but if that had changed, since that had changed, shouldn't it have been him?

This was typical —Roy let them do the work, and then he moves in for the kill. Which is how B. saw this, saw Jeanette—"Ned" now. She was even using Roy's nickname. Though B. saw her in tears, eventually. Even if Roy married her.

Especially if Roy married her. Which he overheard Rhonda complaining to Mel might take place. Roy was rarely home for dinner those days, and never on weekends. Even Sunday nights—it seemed that Ned's parents had decamped to Florida for the winter, so the coast was clear for Roy to pick up a pizza pie from the Venetian Room, a rare treat in those days, and take it over to her house for her children. The oldest one, the girl, was twelve or thirteen, gangly still but you could see the looks behind it. Like her mother—although the girl's father was good-looking too, and on his third wife. Lucky for the kids that he never came around.

Roy told Rhonda that they would sit in what they called the library in front of the fire and watch *Bonanza*. The girl would eat her pizza and then vanish—"homework," her mother explained, but Roy suspected she didn't like her mother smiling back at "Uncle Roy." That was all right with him—he even appreciated it. Appreciated her resistance, her great wall. He would breach it. He asked her about her schoolwork, her favorite subject—French—and brought her a red heart-shaped box of candy for Valentine's Day. Caught her off-guard with that, and she gave him an open smile. After that, he could smile back at her, though she'd still make herself scarce after a piece or two of pizza.

"Uncle Roy"—why not? He brought his daughter, about the girl's age, to town to visit and she was nice to her. They played cards together—some version of rummy—and she took her along with her friends to the movies. Afterward, they came running back to Ned's house—they'd seen *The Birds* and were afraid that the crows in the maples were swarming to attack. That night, as Roy was driving her back to Cleveland, his daughter asked him if he was going to marry Ned.

"Should I?" he asked, with his smile.

"Yeah!" said the girl. "Then we could all live here together."

Roy asked what Ned's daughter thought.

"She wants you to."

Roy took it in. He'd done all right there, then. Captured the castle.

"We all do," said his daughter, but did he, Roy? Did Ned?

Granted, she had become a social outcast, almost, in this

provincial town, since her divorce, but she was beautiful and cultured and from a different world from theirs, the Whites'. She belonged still, probably on her parents' membership, to the good country club, while they, even now that they could afford it, hadn't even tried to get in. They'd joined the new one, which, despite the second-rate golf course, they liked better anyway. Where they felt at home.

He'd taken her there once for a big-deal Saturday night lobster dinner, but saw then that it probably wouldn't work. She knew everyone, but didn't have a friend among them. They were the girls she hadn't talked to at school, the boys who'd known not to even think of asking her out. The fact that she was there that night with Roy White instead of her ex-husband, a man from her own circle, had laid out her own status—"down a peg"—for the world to see. She was a good sport, though, smiled and chatted with everyone, laughed and struggled like they did with the lobsters, but he could see she was faking it. This wasn't her first lobster.

So how would it go with them, if it did go? It wasn't as if he was close with anyone there either; growing up he hadn't had time to make friends, or the inclination, eventually. He actually preferred the crew who worked for them at the yard.

A few months later, he took her home for dinner. Rhonda was going to make steaks and her potatoes, but then decided, why take the risk? She ended up getting cold cuts from the deli. Coleslaw. Pickles. Nothing personal if Ned didn't like it. There were soft drinks, and Mel mixed seven and sevens. Roy knew Ned liked scotch, but she took Mel's drink with a smile. She was a good sport, no question. A nice person, even Rhonda was thinking as the night wore on. Didn't talk too much, or try to show off. Drop names, or hint that she was slumming—just the opposite. Seemed to like being there. Seemed especially to like Roy.

And he, her. Roy was wearing a big-deal shirt, baggy pink oxford cloth, that she'd brought him from Brooks Brothers in Pittsburgh. *Who the hell in this house has even heard of Brooks Brothers?* B. felt like saying. And who in this house wears pink shirts, for Chrissake?

They were laughing, joking—Roy looking ridiculous, like an overgrown schoolboy in that shirt. B. watched them for a few minutes and then put down his head and ate. Like that. "Ate"—didn't "have dinner." That too had come up. Just as Mel was saying, "Let's eat," Rhonda spoke over him, something she rarely did—she liked Mel's ways—and said, "Let's have dinner."

B. had looked up, but he knew where it was coming from. That time Roy had brought Ned home on their way, as Ned had put it, "out to dinner." Not "out to eat." No one had said anything at the time, but they'd all taken note, clearly. So now it was "have dinner" instead of eat, but not for B. Anyway, he had to go, he said, as he pushed his plate back.

My ass, Rhonda could see Mel thinking, but thank God didn't say. B. disappeared upstairs for a few minutes, then came down and with a wave went out the door. Ned smiled and waved, but turned back to the table, to Roy. Afterward, they played a few hands of gin, with Ned feeling her way. She had never played four-handed, she admitted with a laugh.

"So what do you play, bridge?" asked Mel.

But Ned said that bridge had never really interested her. She didn't mention the fact that she had started teaching— full-time, high school English. And what with the children, there wouldn't have been a lot of time left for a leisurely bridge game. She looked wonderful that night, her long dark hair shining, done in what they called a long pageboy. A nice sweater and slacks.

But Rhonda had seen her at the A&P a few weeks earlier, late one afternoon, and she'd looked worn out, "beat," clearly, after work. Her hair hung lank, her dress was wrinkled. She was buying Cream of Wheat, English muffins, canned fruit. Rhonda ducked back into an aisle, and didn't say hello. She didn't want to call forth one more effort from her that day.

But here she sat, playing cards with them, catching Roy's smiles, returning them, and as soon as they could, leaving together. Oblivious, it seemed, to the hurt that had sat across the table earlier. Did she even remember that she'd once snubbed B.? It was twenty years ago, but yesterday to B., Rhonda was seeing. Ned was still his girl, in his dreams, at least. He was her age, in his thirties, nice-enough-looking, eligible surely. When had he last even had a date? And how would he take it if Ned married Roy?

But would she marry Roy? Or maybe more to the point, would Roy marry her? Now that Rhonda thought about it, it made no sense either way. Ned's old friends were all college-educated, the men professionals, the women "history majors" who now led book drives and the PTA. Ladies' Golf at the club. Whatever. None of them even knew her, Rhonda's, name. Would Ned take such a leap? For Roy?

True, he had that smile, but what did they talk about? Did they talk? Roy, like B., was a great dancer, but Ned once admitted that she didn't really like to dance. But what did she like? That Roy liked? That was the question, and Rhonda wasn't the only one asking it.

A night or two later, when the three of them, Rhonda, Mel, and B., were sitting in front of the TV, Mel allowed, just casually, apropos of nothing, that a woman who didn't like to dance couldn't be much in the sack.

B. jumped up. "What?"

"I was just saying—"

"There is no sack there!" B. had his finger in his older brother's face. That had never happened before. "No sack."

Rhonda came and sat on the arm of Mel's easy chair and said that she agreed. "Doesn't feel that way to me either."

"Oh come on," snorted Mel. "She's not a schoolgirl."

"She's a teacher," said Rhonda. B. had turned red. He was usually quite pallid, with nice eyes, though. Almost blue, from his mother. He'd supposedly had red hair, when he was little. His father used to call him *"Rot."* Red.

"Teachers don't fuck?" said Mel.

"Melvin!" said Rhonda. It was the first time she'd heard him—or anyone—use that word.

"How 'bout all those teachers' kids, pulling in all the A's in school? Remember them?" Mel continued. "How about her own kids?"

"She doesn't fuck Roy, okay, Mel?" said B., standing too close. Still red.

"How do you know?" said Mel.

"Because he would have told me. Told you too. Told his friends. Told the girl at Tod's"—the lunch place—"told the guys up and down the yard. They'd know, all of them."

That seemed right, actually, and it was a better argument than hers, thought Rhonda. She didn't have to add a word.

Still, she was worried. Maybe Ned was holding out, playing it cool? In order to force the question, but would he ask? She wasn't illegal, immoral, or fattening—no one could call her Roy's type. True, she was a catch, would be, if he landed her, but what then? Rhonda couldn't see it working out, whichever way she turned it. Would he join the good country club on her membership, and take up golf, sit by the pool with people he barely knew, smoking his big cigar? But those country club men didn't smoke cigars, they were tall and trim and had gone from high school together to Ohio State or down to Athens, and joined the same fraternities. Roy was short and getting fat, and you could never mistake him for one of them, no matter how many Brooks Brothers shirts Ned put on him.

Which would leave it to Ned to be the one, should they decide to try to make a go of it together. Embark, she'd have to, on a permanent slumming expedition—join the cigar set, where no one would be sporting Greek letters, or reading *Catch*-22, or watching *Dick Cavett*, even, both of which Rhonda had heard her mention lately. But Roy's friends weren't readers, and late-night TV was for people who didn't have to be out at an auto wrecking yard at six a.m.

Roy mentioned one night that he and Ned were going to an art show at the local museum—for that pop artist who took bits of the comics and blew them up. It was a big deal, apparently, though Mel thought his work was a joke on the suckers, and Roy had to agree.

But he went with her and even met the artist, who'd been a fraternity brother of some of Ned's friends, back in Columbus. Rhonda found a photo of them on Roy's bureau, snapped that night, a Polaroid. Ned, glamorous in a black dress, smiling, and Roy too, but not his million-dollar smile. More like fifty cents.

And then soon after, in a turn of the wheel, Roy invited her to a costume party. Rhonda and Mel were going too, as the farmer and his wife, but Ned had come dressed as a beatnik, her hair long and straight, in a long black sweater, beret, and black tights, a novelty then. She looked fabulous, Rhonda thought, but also like she was at the wrong party, where no one even knew what a beatnik was. There was another Polaroid—women with beehive hairdos dressed like Playboy bunnies or milkmaids, the men, including Roy, some version of cowboys, and Ned, to the side, looking toward the door. B., a cowboy too, looking at Ned.

Caught, all of it, in that little photo. Roy put it up on the mantel, but after a few days, Rhonda tore it up and took it out with the garbage. Could Ned marry Roy? And if she did, what would become of them, the brothers? Even the yard? Maybe B. would have to walk away, which might seem all right to Mel and Roy at first. Until they saw that he was the glue that held the rest of them together. The one who slipped the more desperate employees the extra fiver when Mel and Roy wouldn't have, and saved the brothers the trouble of starting over with a new guy. The one who bred in his own quiet way a sort of loyalty, as far as that could go in a junkyard.

Rhonda was thinking that without B., there might not be the White brothers either. No way Mel and Roy could get along without that buffer. B. was the youngest, had grown up deferring to Roy, although now, with Ned, that modus vivendi was fraying. Whenever she showed up now, B. would "have a date" and go out, even if it was late. Even if it was Sunday night and snowing, and they were settled into *Ed Sullivan*. Roy wouldn't say anything, just watch him go—Rhonda too. She didn't want to have to sit there either, making conversation with this woman who seemed to hold their fate in the palm of her hand, and who had never had a word for any of them till she started falling for Roy.

Not, in fairness, that their paths had crossed much. Rhonda was from Monongahela, a small coal mining town twenty miles from Pittsburgh—a long twenty miles, though. Her father had been the town druggist, so she'd grown up on the right side of privilege there. They even had a girl down from the hills to help her mother in the house, and Rhonda had been expected to finish high school.

But no one there had ever thought of college, and then the war came, and she'd met a guy from Youngstown, married him before he shipped out, and moved there with him after the war. It had seemed okay at first—anything would have, after the grim gray streets of her world till then. Youngstown was growing, booming, her husband got work as a bookkeeper for one of the mills, and was making enough so that she didn't have to work at first. She got to know the parks then, Mill Creek especially, with its meadows and its caves, "Bears Den," as one of them was called, and she felt it there, not the bears so much as the link to way back, as she once tried to tell her husband.

"Like when?" He looked up from the radio. The ball game. The Cleveland Indians, who never, ever won. That much she knew already. Her team was still the Pirates. Pittsburgh. A better bet.

But as for telling him about the spell, the magic she felt in the park by herself during the week, when no one was around, she didn't try again. He'd grown up here, but didn't seem to have many friends, and the only woman she'd met so far was the girl who worked at the corner store where she went every day for the paper and her gum and cigarettes, but that girl never had any time off weekdays to walk in the park, and probably had other things to do on Sundays, when Rhonda's husband was out watching the game somewhere.

Still, Rhonda had grown up a solitary girl, the only one in her class whose father didn't work in the mines, the girl whose parents had the first electric refrigerator in town, which meant that the ice man—who knew all the other children—didn't know her name. She would have been all right with her morning walks alone for a while, forever, even—she was coming to know the birds, particularly the mockingbirds, who she'd never heard before, not where she'd grown up. There was a man there one day with binoculars who told her that mockingbirds had come this far north just recently, since people started planting those rose fences—*Rosa multiflora*, he told her. As if she would know one rose from another.

But she went to the library and looked them up. The man had said that they were a weed, brought in from Asia a hundred years ago, maybe more, and were out of control now. "A plague," he'd said.

Still, she liked them, and the mockingbirds too, who'd followed them north. They sang all of May, into the night too, like nightingales, which she'd imagined but had never heard. Just read about in a poem they'd been given in high school.

She was even thinking, around then, of maybe trying to do something along those lines, take a course at the college, maybe. It was only about thirty dollars a semester— she might ask for that for Christmas instead of anything else. Maybe learn about the birds and the flowers. Biology.

Botany. Subjects that sounded boring till someone told you about mockingbirds and *Rosa multiflora*.

She was thinking of using her own money, and starting that summer, though it was around then that she discovered that her husband had actually lost his job a few months earlier, for "fiscal irregularities" that kept showing up in his accounts. Another "bad apple," as her mother would have put it. But by the time he went bankrupt and signed her name, too, to bad checks all over town, her mother was "gone," and her father too. There was no one left in Monongahela to go home to. So she filed for divorce, moved to a rooming house, and found work in the office of a used car lot, the only place that would hire her.

Which was where she met Mel. He'd come in to assess some old junkers they'd given up on and were selling for scrap, and she had made out the order. She hadn't really noticed him, but he said something funny about the old cars, how he hoped he didn't get them mixed up with his new Cadillac, and she'd looked up and lit a cigarette. He smiled, nicely, shyly, probably the only kind of smile that would have worked with her in those days. Said he'd be back for something or other in a day or so, and she actually went down to Woolworth's and bought the pearl earrings—fake, but they dressed things up all the same. Her hair was short, always, since her schooldays. Once she cut it, she never went back.

But still, the earrings were nice, kind of fun, and she wore them to work for three days in a row before he came back in. Afterward, he told her he'd noticed, and that's what had given him the idea that if he asked her to dinner, she might say yes. Which she did.

It didn't take too long for them to make up their minds. They were both well versed in bad bets. Any puerile dreams of love had given way, in both cases, to a solid appreciation of other virtues. One night at dinner, Mel had asked her about her first husband. To their mutual surprise, tears had started down her face at that.

She hadn't cried yet, she realized, about her first marriage, hadn't dared. She was simply too alone for that. But Mel took her hand, nodded, and listened. He was a man of few words, but she could read sympathy in his small smile, and they came to the understanding that night, that they both considered real trust between two people as the highest form of marital bliss. Mel already had his son. Rhonda said she'd be fine with a small dog.

They got married in Mill Creek Park, outside of Bears Den. It was fall and the mockingbirds weren't singing, but Rhonda was almost glad of that. There were feelings around those evocative songs that she was happy to leave there, in the park. She never went back.

She quit her job at the car lot and started to work at Cleveland Auto Wrecking. She moved into the house with the other two White brothers, into one of the back bedrooms, since Roy had the master and didn't make any mention of moving out. Which was okay with her, everything about that house was okay with her, especially since Mel had gotten her a dachshund, which both Roy and B. seemed to like. As for her, she loved the dog, named him "Jay-zee," after the hot dog stand in town. When he ran into the street and was hit by a car, B. went straight out and got her another one. This one he named "Poncho," and Rhonda kept him on a leash. When they moved to L.A., he was still alive, and Rhonda took him.

*   *   *

The future. Their lives, meanwhile, revolved around the yard, where they all worked, lunch at Tod's steak shack, and then whatever dinner that Willie Mae had ready. Mostly steak and potatoes, or spaghetti and meatballs, iceberg lettuce with Wishbone dressing. What people were eating then and there. Canned peaches for dessert—Ohio in the sixties. Not much conversation during dinner, just some talk about this or that at the yard. Some stolen hubcaps.

The new guy, B. was thinking, but Rhonda had her eye on one of the older ones. The man who'd asked her for an advance—he didn't say for what. She told him no, of course no, it was always no, except once in a while with B. And then he'd make up the difference from his own pocket when the guy he'd taken pity on used the money to skip.

Not that it was ever a lot of money, but one thing they all knew, Rhonda included, was the value of the nickel and the dime. One on top of the other. Knew it was how they were in the nice old house on Gypsy Lane, big enough for all of them, with a room for Willie Mae—small change. Dollars and cents, coming in, one after the other, and nothing much going out. That, too.

The truth was, life was good there then, and not just for the White brothers, but for most of the good solid citizens in those middle-sized towns in America in those days. Post-WWII. Pre-Vietnam. When the kind of questions people were asking had answers, tried and true. Fair and square. When the rich men in town drove old American cars, and made more money, but not enough to push their workers into misery. When no one who wasn't on some sort of crazy quest worked two jobs. When the word "homeless" was twenty years away, waiting for Reagan's attack on the infrastructure to enter the American lexicon.

V

That spring would settle it, Rhonda figured. Ned and Roy would get married or they wouldn't. She mentioned that to Mel, who threw in another alternative: that they might not get married in spring, but still might get married. Come summer. Or fall—"Why only spring?"

And he was right. Spring rolled into summer and then fall, but there still seemed to be no conclusion in sight.

Roy got a new car, a stunner, the new Eldorado Biarritz convertible, the first one in town, cream-colored, even the leather seats. Cream wool rug on the floor. He took Ned and Rhonda for a ride—the three of them across the front, top down, Ned in the middle. It was a beautiful September day, warm enough to stop for frozen custard, and Ned had chocolate. The scoops were enormous, and Ned's ended up dripping on the carpet. Roy screeched to a halt and hopped out.

"Get out," he barked to the two women. He pulled out his handkerchief, spat on it, and started scrubbing the blond wool.

"I can get it out at home—" Rhonda began.

Ned apologized, but added, "It's just a car."

Roy looked up at her with shock in his eyes—anger too. Just a car? He couldn't even speak, for a moment.

Rhonda was shocked as well—how could Ned say such a thing to Roy, to any of the White brothers? Their lives were cars—Cleveland Auto Wrecking, for heaven's sake. What was she thinking? No car was "just a car" to them—at the yard, a car was either a wreck or a salvage, but their livelihood, either way. As for their own cars, they were a form of self-portrait. Some version of who they were, the one they could control.

Ned should have known this, Rhonda was thinking, how could she not know? Should have sensed it, or at least read about it. With her college education, her teaching, her reading. Her art exhibits, her culture—but what about some basic human nature?

Or had it been deliberate? Her way of telling him no. There was a moment then, just a beat, really, when Roy and Ned stood there, staring at each other like strangers. Long enough for Rhonda to think, *So maybe not.*

"Look," she said, "it will be all right, trust me. Soon as we get back, I'll get out the Fels-Naphtha," and so on, and Ned promised she would never eat ice cream in his car again.

"Unless it's vanilla," said Roy, and with tight smiles all around, they got back in the car and drove on.

But that Sunday night, Roy brought his pizzas home instead of to Ned's house, which Rhonda took as a good sign, given her allegiances—the brothers, *über alles.* But when the two of them, she and Roy, took the pizzas into the living room, to eat in front of the TV, Mel was in one of the easy chairs, and B. had the other one.

Roy decided to take on B. "Hey, you're in my seat," he said.

"Oh yeah?" said B., turning red but not taking his eyes from the screen.

Roy glared at him. Rhonda recalled the story of Sam White's own brother, the brick at his back, nearly killing him.

"It's B.'s now, Roy," she said lightly, "unless you really want it back. And we can get another one. If you're going to be here—"

"I'm not going to be here," said Roy, and he walked out the door.

"Least he left the pizza," said Mel, and they went back to their TV, though B. didn't eat his till it had gotten cold.

Roy came back late, after they were in bed, but Rhonda heard him and whispered to Mel that she would bet money that he'd gone to the Lamppost and not to Ned's. But Mel said he only bet on horses, not women.

Nor, he added, did he care.

Still, he should care, said Rhonda, didn't he care about Cleveland Auto Wrecking? Did he want a rift among the White brothers over a woman?

"Why a rift? She's never even looked at B.," said Mel, which was true, but irrelevant. But as Rhonda started to explain, Mel drifted off and soon was snoring, and she decided that maybe she could leave it at that. Since maybe— maybe—they had both paused, Roy and Ned, and thought about it. Which, she figured, would be fatal.

A month or so later, there was a shooting at the yard. Some crazy guy who'd taken a lot of trouble salvaging a part from a wrecked car had brought it in, thinking he'd earned some good cash. But Roy lowballed him, and he flipped out, pulled a gun, and shot him. More shot at him, since he only grazed the side of Roy's arm, and then panicked and ran, throwing the gun down behind him.

"Thank God!" said Sheri, who was sobbing in the corner.

"A-men," said Mel, though what he was thankful for was that Rhonda was out that day.

B. said he'd drive Roy to the hospital, but, "Nah," said Roy, "it's only a scratch"—which was true, said Sheri, after she washed and bandaged his arm. The real question was whether to call the cops. B. argued against it. They'd find the guy, throw him in the can for a few days or weeks, but then he might come back. This way, he was probably scared off.

"He tried to kill me!" Roy protested.

"Yeah, but you were cheating him," said B.

"Bullshit!" Roy got to his feet. "Guy shoots me, and you're taking his side?"

"It wouldn't have happened if you'd given him the right price."

"So it's my fault?"

They were staring at each other. If Rhonda had been there, she would have stepped in, but Rhonda wasn't there, and Mel never stepped in to anything.

"You brought it on! Fucking cheating the guy!"

"You're crazy. Jealous—"

B. grabbed his shirt—Roy flinched back. "My arm—"

B. moved away. "Sorry."

"Damned right," said Roy. And he went back to his desk and B. walked out to the far end of the yard. He found a half cigar he'd left there a few days before, and lit it, breathed in too deep, coughed, and took a breath. This was his life. Not much, but what else was there? Later that evening, he called a friend who had a used car lot on Mahoning Avenue, and the two of them booked a trip to Vegas. The room at Caesar's was comped, since they'd been there before and lost enough in the casino to be worth it. That was fine with B., though. Sure, he'd drop a little cash, maybe on the girls, too, after a show. The point then being to get away from Roy before he himself picked up a brick.

Still, Roy didn't seem to be seeing Ned so much anymore, or at least he wasn't bringing her by the house, and Rhonda was pretty sure that once she was out of the picture—if she was out of the picture—then life among the brothers would settle back down, to the way it had always been. Roy calling the shots, Mel indifferent, B. holding it all together. Roy would take up with some other girl, maybe younger, someone he wouldn't even think about marrying. Someone he'd never bring home.

But as for B., it was funny that he still didn't have a girl-friend, at least that Rhonda knew about. He went out now and again, but always came home earlier than Rhonda had expected.

"How was it?" she'd ask.

"Okay," he'd say, and sit down beside her for the end of Groucho or Jackie Gleason. The only time she saw him laugh.

Was that enough for him? Rhonda wondered. Would he be willing to go through his whole life like that? No wife, no children, barely a chair to call his own.

Not that it was all bad—he had his meals cooked, his bed made, he lived in a nice house with his brothers and with her, who, she truly felt, he loved too, like a sister. A version of family life, though once removed. The yard was growing, business was good. They were making money. No way they would lose this house—they'd already paid off the mortgage, ahead of schedule. If he kept his head down around Roy—easier without Ned in the picture—then there was no reason things couldn't continue as they were, on a rise for the White brothers, along with much of the rest of America in the sixties. And maybe that would do it for B.

On New Year's Eve of that year, Rhonda was surprised to come down and find Ned having a drink in the living room with Roy. They were on their way to a party—his friends this time, and she was wearing a red dress that looked new, maybe bought for the occasion. Flashier, tighter than what she usually wore. Her smile seemed brighter too—she was making a play, Rhonda figured. She had made up her own mind, and now it was all with Roy. If she dripped chocolate ice cream in his car this time, she'd be the one frantically rubbing the carpet.

Roy was jovial, and expansive as well. Having a better time than Rhonda had seen in a while. Now it would happen, she could see it. They had both drawn back and decided that though perfect it wasn't, good enough it maybe was. Better than anything else in that town.

Rhonda was afraid that that night—what with the red dress, which looked fabulous with Ned's dark hair, done in an updo, like Roy's friends' wives, she noted—would be the night. They would turn to each other at midnight, and he would, drunkenly, impulsively, say, *Will you?* and she would, drunkenly, impulsively, say, *Yes*. And that would be the end of the White brothers.

"Thank God," she said to Mel, "that B.'s not home." He'd gone to Pittsburgh with a friend who knew a couple of "gals," as he put it, whom they were taking to dinner and a show. He'd rented a tux and polished his black shoes. Rhonda had noticed but hadn't said anything. Was hoping.

Because if Roy was getting married, it would be good if B. did too, or at least met someone he could marry. Someone he liked enough to forget about Ned. Because that would never be, no matter what. Mel was right. Ned had never even looked at B.

VI

If the red dress had done it on New Year's Eve, Roy wasn't talking, at least not to Rhonda, and January rolled out bleak, cold, with snowdrifts piling up on the golf course across from their house. Maybe he'd asked her, and she'd said no—despite the dress and the hairdo. Maybe that was her way of saying goodbye. Roy wasn't home much for dinner with the rest of them, but whether he was out with Ned or not, Rhonda had no clue. He wasn't talking, and when he smiled at Sheri at the yard one day, it occurred to Rhonda that she hadn't seen that smile in a long time. She missed it.

Because whatever Roy's relationship to B., or to Mel, for that matter, whom he mostly just ignored—probably ever since he was born—he brought a certain dazzle to her own life. That smile. His jokes. Even the stingers. Not that she would ever even dream of fooling around with Roy, but she wasn't about to deny a certain little quiver when it was just the two of them. When he would look at her, actually look, as no one else did, compliment her on her hair—short, graying, not like Ned's, but sometimes, when she'd had it cut and curled, he'd notice. Or a new sweater, and she would feel it, not just hear it. Find herself smiling, almost shyly, and then decide that if he asked Ned to marry him, she would say yes, who wouldn't?

A month or so later, Roy was driving to Cleveland, to take his daughter to dinner, or so he claimed, though Mel doubted that. *He's got something going up there*, Mel figured— immoral, illegal, a girl or a deal that he wanted to keep on the side. Anyway, he was coming home that night, late, and outside of Chagrin Falls he hit a deer and totaled his car. Completely. When they saw it, Mel and B. were astounded that Roy had walked away unscathed. If the car hadn't been solid steel, he would have "booked it for sure," as one of the guys in the yard put it. They'd all stood around, silenced, when Ben White hauled it in.

"Bambi did that?" one of the guys muttered. It seemed impossible—the car looked as if it had been hit by a freight train and left on the tracks for the next one.

"A total wreck," said Ben White.

"Me too," Rhonda thought she heard Roy say, though when Mel asked him, "What?" he'd shot back, "Nothing!"

"Exactly," said B.

They got him a used Caddy to drive around, but it would be a while, the Cadillac people said, till they could get him another Eldorado—the color, that cream, was the rub. Roy complained about the loaner. It was a four-door, and GM-blue. "An old man's car," he said to Mel.

"A rich old man," Mel answered, which true. Although the WASPs in town still drove their rattletrap Country Squires, the newer money rolled around, at about twenty miles per hour, in their four-door Cadillacs, just like Roy's. The same bad blue.

It bothered him. Not much, but enough so that when their mother called one Sunday and mentioned that the old man could use a little help on some land he was buying in Palm Springs—"More rubble," she said—he asked her how big the lot was.

"He won't tell me," she answered.

A bad sign. That meant that he wasn't sure about the deal. She went on to say that she'd gotten a ticket the other day on the freeway, "for driving too slow! Can you believe it?"

Roy could. He said he could see it—his mother toddling along in the Buick in the fast lane, doing thirty.

But, "It's not a Buick anymore," she told him. "Your father drives a Lincoln now."

A good sign. Sam White wouldn't throw away money on a car if he didn't have more where that was coming from. So what was going on out there?

"What were you doing on the freeway anyway?" he asked his mother.

"Going for a ride."

Roy looked out the window. It was still bleak, with the snow blowing off the drifts, across the golf course. It was almost March, but they hadn't seen the sun for weeks. He'd had to fight an unwillingness to go to work the last few weeks, ever since the shooting. It was "nothing," true, but it had unnerved him. That and the car crash.

Though maybe it was all for the best. A chance for him to hit the brakes with Ned, leave the day-to-day at the yard to Mel and B., and take a few weeks out West. Get the lay of the land out there, and see with his own eyes what their father was up to. Who knew but that it might not be a good place to park some of the White brothers' money, instead of at the Mahoning National, where it was piling up. He was just a boy when the bank took their house, but he remembered it. He told his mother he'd call a travel agent and be out the next weekend.

He invited Ned for a drink, and mentioned his trip casually. He hadn't seen her since the car crash, and she looked pretty good. Very good. He'd forgotten how good.

That was the funny thing about her. With some women you remembered, but with Ned he was surprised every time. But why? he wondered. Why did he remember her wrong? As less pretty—was it something to do with the way she'd danced, the few times they'd gone out to nightclubs, stiff, missing the steps? Did that stick, so that he saw her in his mind's eye as flat-footed? Graceless?

Which she wasn't—she was just uptight. All those North Side girls were, and it meant too that she wasn't a tart, wasn't a show-off, which was all to the good. But was she for him? A woman who didn't like to dance?

He was going out to see his parents, he told her, and she looked up, surprised, but didn't ask any questions. No "when's," or "how long's." She just turned toward him in the car and studied his face. He realized she hadn't taken that kind of look at him before, head slightly on the side, eyes narrowed. Assessing—she'd never done that before. She'd left it till then to be the one assessed.

It was as if a veil had lifted between them. She took no trouble to compose her own face, to smile. Just looked at him hard, "man-to-man," he would have said afterward to a trusted confidant or a shrink, if he'd had one. Might have told them that his own call now was "Game over," at least on her part. He himself had hoped to leave it at "Maybe."

But when he took her home that night, there was no kiss, and he remembered afterward that she'd said goodbye, not good night.

Two days later, Rhonda drove him through snow flurries to the airport, outside of town, in Vienna, pronounced Vye-enna, for one of those Ohio reasons. "You think it will fly?" she asked him, yet again. But they'd called just before leaving the house, and the airlines people had said yes, they'd get through "the weather" here, but he had to change planes in Chicago, and who knew from there? He didn't care. He'd sleep in a bad motel or even the airport if he had to. Ever since that last night with Ned, he couldn't get out of town fast enough. Away from the nagging feeling that he'd made the mistake of his life.

But to get on a plane and fly above the clouds—nothing beat it for leaving it all behind. Which was exactly what he intended to do. And when he landed in Chicago, they told him that the L.A. plane was delayed, but they could get him on one just leaving for Vegas. From there, it was a simple hop to L.A.

"Perfect," Roy decided. So it was working out after all. The whole thing—the shooting, the crash, Ned's cold, hard look, all moving him from the freezing sleet and snow to the sun. If you looked at it that way, it all fell into place. He took the flight to Vegas, where he stayed for a few days, lost some money, but ended up hitting with the slots, rented an Eldorado, and cruised through the desert to Palm Springs.

It had gotten bleak fast—sand on either side of the road with tough little tufts of grass poking through—at least, he'd thought it was grass till he'd bent to pick some and sliced his finger. The sign said PALM SPRINGS before anything changed—still the sand blowing across the road, though the mountains were closer. "Rubble," they looked to be, just like his mother had said, only vertical, looming up. No pine trees like mountains were supposed to have, nothing but rocks and gray—rubble.

Was it supposed to be beautiful? Roy turned up the main drag, Palm Canyon, and tried to remember what he'd been expecting—the palm trees, yeah, but these were tall and skinny, or else short with a sort of bunch on top, like a clown's hat. He glimpsed the turquoise of the pools beyond the chain link surrounding the motels, but they seemed to be empty, all of them. Where were the girls in their bikinis? The tanned boys waiting outside to park your car?

It was midday, and Roy realized that his head was pounding. There was a Holiday Inn, but why waste twenty bucks when there was a Motel 6 across the way? He checked in, paid his six dollars, and fell across the mattress in his clothes. When he awoke, it was six in the morning and the sky was a shade of pink he'd never seen. Tinged with purple, and when he went out, he saw the mountains, chill blue against it.

He went into an all-night coffee shop, and after some bacon and eggs, and his third cup of coffee, *Okay*, he thought, *maybe there's something*.

And it turned out there was.

A year slipped by, and Roy didn't come back. That was fine with B. and Mel. The yard continued to do so well without him that B. was even wondering what the hell Roy had done when he was there, besides overcharging and under-paying on valuable parts. They stayed in touch, though—a call on those Sundays when Roy was visiting "the folks," as Rhonda called them. He was working with their father, and one day that fall, he called the yard during the week—prime time, an expensive call, something the Whites didn't do. B. and Mel feared bad news.

But it was good news, said Roy. He was recommending an investment. He wanted them to go in with their father on some of those scrub acres their mother had been wor-rying about.

"Where?" asked Mel. "Palm Springs?"

"No. You got a map?"

They didn't.

"It's called Palm Desert."

"Sounds nice," said Rhonda.

"It isn't," said Roy. "Not yet."

He said it was out in the middle of nowhere, but not for long. The old man had just sold some of his Palm Springs "rubble" to a group of Japanese investors for three times what he'd paid for it, and Roy wanted to put that money into more rubble, but out farther, in Palm Desert. And he suggested that they take the White brothers' money out of the Mahoning National Bank, and come out and have a look at what was happening out there.

"You in?" Roy asked Mel. Mel had never said no to Roy in his life, nor did he want to be the classic fool who missed the money train. The butt of those kinds of stories.

Still, he temporized. "We were thinking to buy some more land here, expand the yard," Mel said. Business was good there. Solid.

"Forget about it," said Roy. "That town is over. This is where to put your money."

"Maybe," said Mel, "probably, yeah," but after he hung up, he sat down with Rhonda and B., and decided that B. should go out and look it over for himself.

B. called Roy before he left. "You want your clothes?" Roy had gone out with just a small suitcase, and left a closetful of slacks and sports coats, shirts, and ties.

"Ties?" said Roy. "No one wears ties out here." Told B. to bring an overnight bag with his underwear and toothbrush, and they'd suit him up when he got there.

B. came back in red checked pants and white shoes, which sat in the closet till his next trip, a month or so later, with a cashier's check for two hundred thousand dollars, the White brothers' down payment for the lot adjacent to the one that Roy and their father had already bought. With that size piece of land, they could move their activities up a notch. Instead of simply selling empty lots to the big guys, they could be the ones to put up the strip mall, or even an office building, depending on the loan that Roy was managing. He had what he called a "relationship" with a banker in Rancho Mirage.

"That really the name of the place?" asked B. He was still wondering if any of it could be real as he handed over the check from back in the land of solid businesses in places with solid names. Roy, though, seemed to have bought the whole deal. He was still his brother, but from another planet now. And their father too—Sam White was drinking carrot juice for breakfast and doing calisthenics with Jack LaLanne on TV.

When he'd first gotten there, B. was shocked to see his father in baby-blue trousers and white shoes, but before long, they'd gotten him tricked out in pastels as well— turned him over to a cute salesgirl in what looked like a golf shop. He'd walked out of there in yellow trousers and a matching Perry Como sweater, because, well, why the hell not? Since he was out there getting rich, trying to, with the rest of them.

"Ohio it's not," said their mother, surveying her menfolk one night as they headed out to supper. She, for her part, had held the line—the same dark baggy dresses as always, the stockings, the little heels.

B. turned and kissed her. "Mama," he said. She gave him one of her comical little looks. Cynical, but with a touch of humor and some small measure of love. Her old self, unalloyed with California.

But when the menu came, he was the one who raised an eyebrow. His mother noticed—"Fancy!" She gave him her shrug. "These days."

Yes, fancy, B. was thinking, but maybe what had changed was less substance than detail, the number of zeros at the end of Sam White's bank account. He was still the good junkman he'd always been, weaving gold from nettles. Million-dollar sales of those acres of rubble.

Not that their illiterate, third-estate father would have described it that way. To him it was simple—he had seen it all his life. Before America even, "over there," where that rubble too had its rich men, the landowners, who fleeced everyone else. Had they been squeamish, centuries ago, when it had come to grabbing the worst land on the continent? Not they, nor would he be, here, on his own continent. He was, one might say, the proper heir to the Ukrainian boyars of his youth, the Terletskys or Lyzohubs, the ones they'd all feared growing up.

Not that he expected them to acknowledge any connection to one of their obscure peasants. Unless they wanted to borrow some cash.

VII

FIVE YEARS PASSED—MUST have, B. realized, when he was driving up the street where Ned lived, and saw her walking down the other side. It was a boulevard, with grass and trees in the middle. Without letting himself think about it, he turned his car around at the end and drove down, stopped beside her, and got out.

She had on a green-striped knit dress, and, with her dark hair, looked flat-out terrific. She was surprised to see him, but not, he thought, unhappy. Not like the first time, when they were seventeen, and she was queen of it all, and he was the poor boy at the frolic.

"Long time," he said, although the question for him was, had it been long enough? The second question, really, since the first one was: Had she been in love with Roy?

If she had been, then five years was nothing. It seemed like nothing to B. right then—what had he done with his life all those years? The yard, money, more money, a few more trips to the desert, to Vegas, none of it touching the thrill he felt right then, standing on the sidewalk of a sedate street in a small town, his heart pounding.

Did you love Roy? he was asking her silently. *Do you still? Was five years enough? If you did, then maybe it wasn't. Maybe you just want to keep walking.* He was watching her eyes. He realized at that moment that she had never quite looked at him before, never bothered to meet his eyes. Just brushed past him with her glance, politely, and past Mel and Rhonda too, on her way back to Roy.

But now she looked at him and smiled, still with some surprise. "Yes," she said, and asked how they all were, Mel, Rhonda. Didn't mention Roy.

But B. did. Said he was still in California.

"Oh, Roy," she said, laughing, and he asked her to dinner that night.

"What time?"

"Seven? Eight?" he said, and she said eight, and they went to the Mural Room, and they both had his veal and scotch and sodas, and she ordered ice cream for dessert.

"What kind?" asked the waitress.

"Chocolate," said B.

Ned looked up at him quickly, then smiled.

He waited till the waitress left, then took her hand. "You can drip it all over my car, anytime," he said.

She looked a little older, must have rounded forty, but so had he. And they both of them, for different reasons, had been on ice for a while, five years, in fact. She because, she admitted to herself that night, she'd been half waiting for Roy. He because he was waiting for her.

And when the chocolate ice cream arrived, they both started laughing, and that was the end of those five years. There she was, out with him, not Roy. There he was, B., not Roy. He asked her no questions, and she told him no lies. But as she ate her ice cream, she started laughing, almost too much, and then so did he, till they were in tears, both of them. They laughed in the car afterward, and laughed as he drove her home. Five years' worth of laughing, that night.

And then they got married.

At least that was their creation myth. But in fact, time wasn't quite the jet plane that B. remembered. Ned was so surprised to see him that afternoon that her first thought was, *Roy's sent him with a message.*

She'd been having a drink with a friend up the street, and was on her way home to a family dinner, with some of her mother's elderly cousins in from Cleveland. She hadn't been actively thinking about Roy for a while, and was, all in all, glad to be rid of him. He was attractive, no question. He knew women, loved women. And if he hadn't left, she'd probably still be seeing him. It might have been beyond her to walk away.

But he was the one who'd walked away, and she was, yes, all in all, glad of it. In fact, she'd gotten to the point where she never wanted to see or hear another word about him again in her life. So when B. drove up that afternoon and asked her to dinner, she pled the family obligation and turned him down, and he drove away.

For the best, she figured, though she mentioned it to her mother.

"What?" said her mother.

"Well, the cousins are here—"

Her mother shook her head. It wasn't as if she too hadn't paid a price through the years. She'd had her own house, set up her own way, with her own furniture, where her friends felt free to call in of an evening. Her afternoon card games with mixed nuts. She'd grown up in Brooklyn. "No peanuts!" it would give her pleasure to tell the grocer.

All this had fallen away, once she had moved to Ned's house—not that she resented any of it. The children had come first, of course, of course. That was the way she and her husband had always lived their lives, and it was, for the most part, a satisfactory solution, both for them and Ned's children. But what about Ned?

Her mother had watched Roy drift off, with relief and misgiving, mixed. She'd noted the smile flitting across Ned's face, the light in her eyes when Roy came around, not that Ned ever said a word to her, they were not confidantes. But still Ned's mother had harbored some hopes there. If he wasn't perfect—she never trusted charmers— still he was something. And without him, there had been nothing. Pretty much nothing.

And now here was his brother, the quiet one, B. Exactly, it came to Ned's mother. She turned to her daughter and said, "Call him back," and Ned did. She told him she was free to go after all, and they'd had what she remembered as some fun, and that laugh—though not quite as definitive as B. recalled it—over the chocolate ice cream.

Nor had it been the seamless glide he seemed to remember, from that laugh to forevermore. B.'s spoken English was junkyard, not country club. He wore black suits where her friends' husbands wore tweed and flannel. He had a gap between his front teeth, and her daughter seemed to hate him. She had liked Roy—he had charmed her. But B. wasn't charming in that way.

Ned knew the girl's objections, but she had at that point been divorced for over a decade. It had been five years since

Roy. Not that she hadn't had some interesting times since then. She'd gone to England, met a man in Parliament, Sir so-and-so, but across the sea proved too far, and then there'd been a lawyer in Pittsburgh, and a doctor in Cleveland too, but they had children of their own, problematic, and she couldn't see it with either of them, in the end.

So what there had mostly been were long evenings of cards with her parents, Monopoly with the children. Weenie roasts in the park, bonfires in the backyard, Girl Scouts, Cub Scouts, *Winnie-the-Pooh*. All of which she loved, *But ten years*, she was thinking.

B. wasn't slick like Roy, but on the plus side, B. wasn't slick like Roy. And unlike Roy , he was slim—so everything he liked wasn't "fattening," and maybe that went for "illegal" and "immoral" as well.

He wasn't good at sports—he'd had no training as a boy with balls or clubs or rackets. But he had a physical grace that went beyond the dance floor. They'd gone to Seven Springs for the day—she was going to teach him to ski, but they ended up getting a room at the lodge instead and not coming out for supper. She'd called her parents to say they were stuck in a blizzard, which wasn't that far from the truth.

Ned still wasn't sure—was this it, then, for her? No English MP? No lawyer or doctor? She had been to New York a few times, bought a hat at Bergdorf's, seen *Galileo* and *Barefoot in the Park*. She'd loved that, but there would be no New York with B., she knew. No Brecht or even Neil Simon. Las Vegas, maybe, or even L.A. Which would be fun—Ned was a good sport, and she would like it. But there were doors and windows that would close if she married B.

But as she was mulling, measuring, hesitating on the

brink, he went to Las Vegas with some friends over New Year's, and Ned sat home alone. Her parents were in Florida, her children out with their friends. When he called at midnight, she was in bed, but raced for the phone. And when he came back the next week, he asked her to marry him.

Or rather, she thought he had. They were standing on the back steps outside, in the cold and the dark, and as he seemed to be asking, he slipped on the ice and snow that Ned's teenage sons were supposed to have shoveled, and fell. Hurt his knee, and had to be helped into the car. And then he drove straight away.

Ned went slowly into the house, angry about the steps, but too overwhelmed to call out the boys. Her daughter, home from college for Christmas, came downstairs in the oversized farmer's overalls she'd been wearing all vacation, held up by a pair of old suspenders. Good thing Ned's father was in Florida. He took personal offense at his grandchildren's clothes those years—the overalls, the tie-dyed T-shirts, a pair of pants made from an American flag.

Ned looked up at her. The girl stopped—"Are you all right?"

"I think Uncle B. asked me to marry him."

"You think?"

Yes, that would have been her daughter's reaction. "Uncle B." could do nothing right, nor did she think her mother was doing anything less than throwing herself away on him. Her own preference had been the Englishman.

On the other hand, she spent most of the year away at college now. Ned's sons were at boarding school.

"Do you love him?" she asked her mother.

Ned took a breath and answered truly, maybe for the last time. "I haven't really thought about it," she said.

They looked at each other. In later years, the girl tried to remember exactly how much of a brat she had been. Did she say something sarcastic then, make one last attempt to stop what she saw as a sorry end to her mother's story? Did she repeat her mother's words back to her? She might have, but hoped not.

Because she knew what those words meant: *I am, to be honest, not in the position to think about love. I have been divorced for more than ten years. I am forty-three now and still good-looking; but when I was thirty-three and better-looking, I received no offers. I was always considered prettier, smarter, more fun than anyone in town, but I haven't been asked to a dinner party since your father left.*

The girl was eighteen then, almost nineteen. She loved her mother, appreciated her beauty and her unfailing high spirits, and still expected her to marry some lord of the manor, which she deserved. To have her marry the owner of the local junkyard instead, who didn't even speak good English—didn't seem right, didn't seem fair. Ned taught grammar! She'd brought them up to despise anyone who said "I" when it should have been "me." The objective case.

The phone rang. The girl usually went for it, but this time she let her mother pick it up. She could hear Rhonda, B.'s tacky sister-in-law, through the phone.

"Congratulations!" Rhonda was saying. So it was true—he had asked, and Ned must have accepted. He'd gone home and told his family. When Ned hung up, she and the girl hugged each other, both of them in tears.

That call had cost Rhonda. She was deeply upset. Mel, though true and steady, was not much for conversation. He was happy to come home from the yard and turn on the TV. She'd even tried, "Let's talk," but, "About what?" was always his answer.

But B. would be full of the news from the yard. The workers' trials and tribulations, the steak-shack guy's recent marriage to the wife of his cook. Ex-wife, but not ex-cook. "Go ahead and take her," the cook had said, and came to work the next morning. Mel just shook his head, but Rhonda had laughed with B.

And now, he would, presumably—obviously—move into the big house with Ned. Rhonda stifled the impulse to suggest that Ned move in with them. She'd come of age knowing you couldn't undo a blow that's come down on your head. No point wasting time trying.

So she picked up the phone and called Ned. And Ned never forgot that call—so it was true! More than just a nice gesture, Rhonda's call was confirmation, and Ned found herself smiling into the phone. Maybe it was true that she hadn't "thought about" marrying B., but now that it was coming to pass, she found herself flooded with warmth and even happiness. Maybe B. wasn't perfect, but neither was she, she told her daughter. Or maybe she didn't, but should have—she couldn't quite remember. Couldn't remember anything from the whirlwind that swept over them all in the next few weeks.

B. and Ned decided to fly to L.A. to get married with his parents. Ned's children were relieved not to have to stand there and fake smiles. Ned's parents came back from Florida and gave a party for them at the club—Ned put together the list. All her old friends, the ones who hadn't invited her all those years. Ned didn't know how to hold a grudge, her mother and her daughter agreed.

But Ned seemed to have put all that behind her. She was married, she was happy, she and B. were made for each other, as of that day when he had asked and she'd said yes. They became a couple among the other couples, invited to every dinner in town.

B. moved in and took over the bills—college and boarding school, too, to Ned's relief, though she hadn't expected it. She really had no idea at first how deep his pockets were, had made no inquiries. She just assumed that together, with her salary and his, they'd do fine. She kept teaching. He'd given her a nice diamond from the local jeweler, and had wanted to buy her a Cadillac, but she demurred. The teachers' parking lot was one step up from Cleveland Auto Wrecking, rusty old Fords, battered Dodge Darts. As it was, she didn't wear the diamond to school, just the gold band that went with it.

Nothing much has changed, being her message, though everyone knew that everything had changed. She was no longer looking tired at the end of the school day. She wore colorful scarves and pearls, and got a new handbag to replace the worn old tote she'd hauled around for years. As for a car, B. came home one day with a red Mustang convertible. Her favorite color. She took the principal out for a spin.

During school vacations, her children came back to pretty much the same furniture throughout the house, but at dinners, there was B. in their grandfather's seat. He didn't say grace or pour water as their grandfather had done, or ask about their classes. Conversation depended entirely on Ned. One night, Rhonda and Mel came to dinner, and Ned's daughter came downstairs in her MAKE LOVE, NOT WAR T-shirt.

Mel had fought in the Battle of the Bulge. "Hey! You try telling that to the Russians!"

"At least the Russians aren't burning babies in Vietnam!" returned Ned's daughter.

And it went from there to, "If you're such a Commie, why don't you move to Russia?" before Ned could get the subject closed. This scene would repeat, with slight variations, the few times Ned brought the two families uncomfortably together in those early, crazy years. B. mostly stayed out of it, though his sympathies lay with Mel, and he'd occasionally allow himself a "These kids!" But he was too nice, and maybe too smart, Ned was coming to see, to criticize them to her.

He'd never had children of his own—and the first thing he did was buy Ned's children new bikes. Ned was surprised by this, but his old neighbors, the Whites, wouldn't have been. They'd have understood the delight in his eyes, as he took a turn on each, even the girl's. She said she was too old for a bike, but it was a black Raleigh with hand brakes, and she couldn't resist it. Took it out early in the morning, when her friends wouldn't see her. Even took it back to college when she left. B. was a little sorry this time to see her go—he'd grown to like the action, the life in the house, when Ned's kids were around, though he wasn't quite at ease with them yet. Especially the girl, but that would come, Ned told him.

She had no doubt about it. She had insisted from the start that the children call him "Dad," though that was awkward for them, and for him too. But Ned was adamant, and none of them, not even her daughter, raised a complaint. They could see their mother was happy. There was a man in the house now too—they'd had their grandfather, but their grandfather was old. One of the boys told his sister that he'd taken the golf club out from under his bed and put it back in the bag.

"You had a golf club under your bed?"

"Yeah, in case of a burglar—"

She nodded at him—"Yeah"—but that night as she was leaving, she called out, " 'Bye, Dad," as she went out the door.

She had her own life by then anyway, and wasn't even in town the next year for another family dinner, this one a farewell. Rhonda and Mel were following Roy to California. The White brothers were reconfiguring under the California sun. It was sleeting that night in Ohio, which must have helped. Because despite it all, this was their home, Mel had been born here, done well here, he knew the place, even liked it, even in the sleet. But it didn't take a weatherman, as they say, to see which way the wind was blowing through that town in those days.

True, Black Monday wouldn't come for another five or six years, when Youngstown Sheet & Tube shut its doors on five thousand steel workers one sunny Monday morning in September—which ended up being fifty thousand jobs lost, once you counted the barbers, the cocktail waitresses, and, eventually, the bankers. In other words, everyone, the population then being about a hundred and fifty thousand.

But even before that, it was no longer looking good. Youngstown was a steel town, and the talk around steel was now Korea. Brazil. People were starting to drive Toyotas instead of Chevys, trading their Cadillacs for new Mercedes-Benzes. Even the White brothers moved on from their Caddies, though just over to Lincolns, not foreign, not yet. But the town still wasn't going anywhere but down. None of their friends' children were coming back after college. It looked like Mel would have to sell the house at a loss.

As opposed to what was going on out in the desert. B., like their mother, had been appalled at first by the scrub acres in the lowly end of the whole Palm Springs region, where their father was conjuring "retail" and gleaming office complexes. But Sam White turned out to be right, and Roy had seen it soon enough for the family to take part in what would be called, straight-faced and all values aside, a real-estate "miracle."

The money they'd put there a few years earlier had almost doubled. When Mel and Rhonda came back from scoping it out before moving, they tried to give Ned a picture of the place. The best part, Palm Springs itself, had been taken years ago, Rhonda explained. Bob Hope, Sinatra, Bing Crosby, even one of the minor Gabors had the houses up against the mountains with the views, and the local Indians seemed to have held on to the palm trees—"Oases," they called them. But Sam White and then Roy had taken the White brothers farther out—no mountains, no palm trees, but still, money to be made. Mel said he had to give them credit for their vision, because from what he could see, it "just looks like hell."

"Not desert like in the movies, with those sand dunes," said Rhonda, but gray, gravelly dirt, with no trees except some spiky things.

"Cactus?" asked Ned. "That can be beautiful—"

"Not even," said Mel.

"Joshua trees," said Rhonda. Apparently they were hundreds of years old. Thousands, some people claimed.

"But ugly," said Mel, although Sam White had seen the potential.

"And who better than a junkman?" put in Rhonda.

"Former junkman," said Mel, but Ned laughed and said Rhonda was right. Who better equipped to see the value of that rubble than the man who'd turned a cart full of trash into the biggest auto wrecking yard in the country, and now the makings of some serious real estate money out in the Golden West?

When Mel left, B. put Cleveland Auto Wrecking up for sale. Ned's house too. It was on the nicest street in town, with three stories and graceful rooms, trees, but all they could get by then was the same thirty thousand dollars she'd paid twenty years earlier, when that was real money.

The wrecking yard, though, went for a decent price— it was still doing well, better than ever, since demand for used parts had risen with the unemployment rate. Once in California, they landed first in a cramped apartment in a building in Glendale that B. had bought a few years earlier, and that had looked nice enough to Ned in the pictures, though when they arrived, the neighbors spoke Spanish and played their boom boxes in the street. When Ned's children came home, all three had to share a bedroom. The youngest boy, whom Ned had enrolled in the local fancy day school, made tracks back to his boarding school in Ohio. The other two conjured excuses and left for college early. An old friend who came to visit called Ned's brother. "Poor Ned," he said.

"Did she tell you her husband owns the whole complex?" asked her brother.

She hadn't. It hadn't even occurred to her to apologize, or clarify. Though her children were appalled, she herself wasn't bothered in the slightest—was, in fact, actually happy to be part of a newly married couple in a crummy little place. It felt as if she and B. had grabbed a chance to be young together.

It was true what she'd said when her daughter had asked if she loved B. She truly "hadn't thought about it." Love was just a four-letter word to Ned. She'd loved her ex-husband, and when he left, she'd nearly gone mad. Once, before she'd told anyone, when she was still hoping, praying, that he'd come back, she spotted him driving in a car with a woman and had madly, insanely, started chasing them—even after he saw her and sped up. But she pursued like one of the Furies, until he turned onto a dirt road and came to a stop. The woman's head had disappeared—she must have hit the floor, like the common slut, the small-time trash that she was. Ned had leapt from her car and, sobbing, screaming, started pounding on his car door, but he hadn't opened it, or even turned to look at her. And finally the madness had broken, and, half-collapsed, she'd groped her way back to her car and driven home.

She got into bed then with a low-grade fever—the kind old woman who worked for her brought toast and tea. She too had been left by a husband she'd loved, long ago, in the coal mining hills of Pennsylvania. She was working for Ned then without pay, as there was no money. Ned's husband hadn't sent any, and Ned didn't want to ask her parents, until she was sure he was gone for good.

Meanwhile, she and Margaret, the housekeeper, cashed in pop bottles and bought spaghetti on credit, and tried to keep the children unaware. But the girl, six or seven by then, started wetting her bed again, and whispered that she kept dreaming that their house was gone. She would be walking up and down on their block, but their house wasn't there.

Ned had dried her own tears then, and got out of bed. Looked in the mirror and asked herself why. Her friends weren't as pretty as she was, weren't as smart—what was it about her that couldn't keep a husband? No one else was divorced—no one. Was she too smart, too dumb? Too fat, too thin? But her friends were fat and dumb, thin and smart, and their husbands loved them. What was *wrong* with her? She and her husband had three beautiful children. They had moved into a house that he had chosen, he had loved. He had paid the top decorator in town, and spent time on the furnishings. She'd thought at first maybe he'd come back for all of that, or even some of it.

But he wasn't coming back. She'd had a glimpse of the woman on the floor of the car—pregnant, Ned had heard. Heard too that he'd gone to the local Catholic bishop to try to get his marriage to her annulled, her three children—his children—declared illegitimate. And meanwhile they were eating boiled spaghetti, since he still hadn't sent them anything to live on.

She finally took her children to her parents' house for dinner, and when the children cheered at the sight of steak, her parents had turned to her, puzzled, and she revealed the shameful truth: her husband had left her. But her parents stepped straight into the breach. Shame? The shame was his! He was a scoundrel, a bounder, not worthy to kiss her feet! As for the children's bad dreams, the parents sold their own nice house, moved into Ned's, and stabilized their world. Paid the bills. Bought groceries. Spaghetti became a treat again. The nightmares ceased.

And Ned resolved to do the sensible thing and become a teacher. She had been enrolled in Indiana University when she graduated from high school, but had eloped instead. It was 1942. Her husband was in the Navy, shipping out to the South Pacific. He was married in his white dress uniform, gloves and all. She had lost her breath at the sight of him.

Then. But now she enrolled in classes at the local college, which she found she enjoyed. She met the few local celebrities who hung around there—the TV announcer, the disc jockey, but had little time for friends once she started teaching high school English in a school outside of town, in the country. She was a colorful bird among the other teachers, many of whom were working farmers, and her students loved her. She rose through the ranks. She never spoke to, or even of, her ex-husband again. Her social life was mostly the children. Vacations were day trips to local spots of interest. Nelson Ledges, where the children learned the word "spelunking." Fairyland Forest, where they gave bottles to baby goats. Burton for maple sugaring and pancakes at the firehouse.

Roy was a break from all that.

He'd woken her up, in fact, from a long winter's sleep, and that was almost enough, but not quite. There was a lot of fun there, not to mention what could never after be mentioned—the lightness, sheer delight, at the touch of his hand on her back—but she realized, finally, that what came first with her, first and foremost, was trust. And that was never on offer with Roy.

Nor did she love him, not really, not enough to take a risk. That came to her clearly just before he left for California. She was tired that day, worn out, driving home from school, though with Roy leaving, the prospect there was fairly bleak. Home to her parents as if she were fifteen with her life ahead of her, and to her children, as if she were married, with a husband coming home with a paycheck and a smile, a hug from male arms. A brochure in his pocket for a trip that summer, somewhere other than Lake Erie. Not, she knew, of course, that there was anything wrong with Lake Erie.

Since that's where she would be taking the children again that summer, to the kind of nice old cottage in Geneva or Madison-on-the-Lake that a teacher could afford on her own. Perfectly nice places, she was telling herself, though it was hard, since she'd worn clothes she didn't like that day. Not that it mattered what she wore, that day or ever, she was just thinking, when a song came on the radio.

That great voice—who was it? This was the local pop station. The Beatles and Motown. Music that generally left her alone. Untouched.

I've had bad dreams, too many nights,
To think that they don't mean much anymore—

Who *was* this? Who else had these bad dreams? That voice went on—

I'd give anything to see you again.

Who else? Who else?

I'd go down on my knees—

Ned had to pull over—*I'd be pleading for you to come back—* tears streaming down her face.

But not for Roy, she realized. For her husband. Former. Ex.

She sat there, by the side of the road in the sleet and the snow alternating. The song was true, she knew it, could swear to it all herself. Since she too would have given "*any-thing*," to see him again. Would have gone down on her knees, maybe even had—but not for Roy White.

She dried her tears and shook her head. She'd been ambushed by that song, it had come out of nowhere, with the kind of passion you were usually safe from on WHOT, her daughter's station. "The Hot Spot." Why it was even on, she couldn't imagine. Background noise, and then that song.

Painful, surprisingly painful, all right, but clarifying too. That passion, that pain, was her past. "A foreign coun-try," as one of the authors she taught had put it. Who? She couldn't remember. It didn't matter. She wasn't going back. She would be smiling when she walked in the door that evening, dressed a little more nicely for class the next day. Which was how her life went for the next five years, with no further stopping by the side of the road in tears, no loosen-ing of the reins, until she married B.

True, you couldn't have called it a marriage of love, not at first. But as time went on, there was a warmth, a glow that grew, and one day, as Ned was packing up some of her old books, she found herself pausing over *Persuasion*, which she'd read and reread, for courage and comfort during her years alone. She remembered hearing that Jane Austen had refused an excellent proposal of marriage at a very hard time in her life because she didn't love her suitor and refused to trust to "love after marriage." At the time, she'd cheered her on, admired her courage, but now Ned felt that maybe Jane Austen had been wrong. True, "love after marriage" was a different kind of love, burnished, perhaps, by gratitude, by life, one might say, but not necessarily tainted for that. Not necessarily spoiled by the fact that two grown-ups are turning to each other at midnight with smiles that are not unmarked with relief.

True, it was different from the first time—she was not eighteen, not on fire. Neither was B. They had both suffered enough of the slings and arrows to know, even treasure, what they had in bed with each other. She had a man and he had a woman, as simple as that. Adam and Eve, back where it had all started. No ex-husbands, no fraternal rivals. No good or bad English, no right or wrong schools. No complaints, nothing even to fight about, ever, why would they?

This, by the way, would hold for the rest of their lives.

B. was spending half the week in the desert at White Brothers Investments, and before long, he and Ned left the apartment in Glendale for a condo in Canyon Estates, one of the first of the gated communities being thrown up around Palm Springs in the seventies. They bought bikes, took up tennis, decorated the living room in pink and green. But eventually they gravitated up the coast, to Santa Barbara and the kind of lovely, big house that Ned had left behind in Ohio, this one white clapboard instead of brick. "The White House," her children called it, after their step father. They brought their friends and eventually their children to swim in the pool and ride the horses in the paddock. Swim far out into the blue Pacific, from the private beach.

And Ned and B.'s life ended up resembling the one she'd probably dreamed of with her first husband. They started to travel with friends—the French canals, Tuscany, even China—and Ned picked up the sort of committee work she'd had to leave behind when she started teaching, eventually becoming chair of the Women's Board at the local museum. She wore a dress to their gala that B. had bought her in Paris; and when she stood to speak, B. had sat beaming. He was proud of her, always. Still half-amazed that he was the one who'd ended up seated by her side.

And happy to trail after her to whatever evenings her activities led to, but he was the one who brought home a story from the museum that night. When he and a friend, another old codger likewise dragged there by his wife, had exchanged a look and risen from the table to step out for "a smoke"—meaning their cigars—a younger man, whose name they hadn't quite caught, leapt to join them.

"Thank God," the younger man breathed, once they got outside. He pulled out his stash and offered them some. "Really good stuff," he said.

"Is that marijuana?" B.'s friend asked.

"Yeh, have some," the younger man answered. A Brit.

B. and his friend declined, and offered him a cigar—which he, for his part, declined, but they all lit up together, and stayed out for as long as they figured they could get away with, laughing and smoking together. Shaking their heads at what their wives had got them into.

Later that night, someone asked B. what he was like.

"Who?" said B.

"Joe Cocker."

"You had a smoke with Joe Cocker?" exclaimed all three of Ned's children in turn. They had to laugh at the thought of Joe Cocker dragged to a provincial museum gala, practically knocking over his chair to break out of there to have a smoke with two old men. They rented a video of *Woodstock* and showed B. his crazy version of "With a Little Help from My Friends." Ned said his wife had been very helpful with the table decorations.

Ha ha. "Life is a mystery," Ned's children agreed. All of it—how B. and Ned had put together such a house, such a life, two people who never should have met, but who ended up as happy as two mortals can be. They lived into a golden old age there together, until, as *The Arabian Nights* tales conclude, "The Destroyer of delights and the Sunderer of societies" came to sunder theirs as well.

VIII

BUT AS FOR Roy—Roy! Nothing Edenic in the cards for him, but then, family happiness had never been his quest. Still, it took him longer than one might have predicted to come to terms with that. To look in his glass and tell the face he viewest that never will that face truly love another.

He hadn't missed a beat when Ned reemerged as B.'s wife. Of course he wanted her back the moment he saw her on B.'s arm. Realized she was the only one for him, the one woman, if any, he could have loved. And wasn't she his, really? Wasn't he the one who'd dug her up, trotted her out, named her, even?

But once that bit of indulgence, that piece of historic revisionism, was behind him, Roy had the sense and, to his credit, decency to treat her like the stranger which he soon found she'd become. There had been one quick moment the first time they came face-to-face—five years!—a question flashing between them.

He: *Are we done?*

She: *Yes. Will you keep your silence?*

He: *Yes. Will you?*

She: *Yes*, and then that was that. The past, buried, or at least rewritten out of both stories.

Which turned out to be easier for Roy than he'd expected. B.'s Ned wasn't Roy's Ned. She was perfectly friendly, but with an underlay of frost. He saw there was not to be an honest word, a real word, between them. And on top of that, she had become cheerful, sporty, fun—all qualities he despised in a woman. Perfect for B., though, who was taking golf and tennis lessons, and riding bikes around Palm Springs with her, with a goofy smile he couldn't seem to keep off his face.

Roy couldn't believe it the first time he saw him, wobbling down the little street on a shiny new English bike, with hand brakes, no less. Way beyond that old black bike their father had revoked, he had said with a laugh, but behind that laugh there was plenty he didn't want to revisit. Their father, at his son-of-a-bitch worst. Their one and only childhood, which hadn't been a childhood. Ned.

And he had to hand it to her—she had also upset the balance of power among the brothers. B. was the youngest, and as such had always been last and least, but now he was the one who'd come home with the prize. Walking into a room with her on his arm had already changed him. Roy had always been the one calling the shots, with Mel nodding yes beside him. But now B. spoke out more in their meetings, and when it came to selling Cleveland Auto Wrecking, he'd made the deal on his own. Presented Roy with a fait accompli.

"You did what?" Roy'd sputtered.

He himself was in the process of selling the yard to someone he knew from the South Side, a local guy who already had a junkyard, when one of Ned's friends, a hotshot lawyer from Cleveland, put together a deal with a buyer from Akron. For twice Roy's price.

Roy was offended, but the Whites didn't argue with money. And with that extra capital, they could buy another parcel he'd had his eye on in Rancho Mirage, and maybe even put up a shopper. Or the kind of office building that you can't do on the cheap, not if you want to get the kind of tenants that would make you rich.

If they stayed together as the White Brothers—that was the thing now. To keep their money together, in the same big pot, which for Roy would mean working with the new B. But the new B. turned out to be better at business than the old B., and at the end of the day, Roy wasn't the man to let personal issues get in the way of a good thing, and he figured that B. wasn't either. They were neither born nor bred to the luxury of that kind of rashness, brothers—business partners—falling out over a woman.

Not that Roy hadn't thought about it, when he heard that B. was marrying Ned. He was visiting his mother the Sunday when she got the call, and his first thought was, *Okay, White Brothers is over.* He never wanted to see either of them again. He hadn't even known they'd been dating.

"I didn't know—" he began to his mother, who didn't say anything, because what was there to say? *What are you going to do about it now?*

The answer to that was obvious: *Nothing.* She brought them all, him, his father, herself even, shots of whiskey. The old folks weren't happy either.

"She's got three kids," said his mother.

"She's divorced," said his father.

Roy drank his drink. Rotgut. Canadian. "Nah, it's okay," he said, and got up and poured himself another shot. Bad stuff. He'd forgotten how bad. "Remind me to bring you a bottle of scotch," he said.

Sam White looked at him. "You know, that time with my brother . . ." He meant the brick that had left him facedown in the dirt sixty years before. It cost him twenty years, he reminded Roy, working alone, to build back up what they lost that day, and as for the brother, he never did much after that. Never pulled himself out of a rental on a back street somewhere on the South Side of town. Sam White wasn't even sure if he was still alive.

It was good, he told Roy, that B. was moving out to California, good for him, and good for the business. "Good to walk into the bank together, all three." Said a team of brothers was something you couldn't buy.

Sam White turned out to be right. Roy was just starting to make inroads with the tall, tanned cowboys who ran the show in the Coachella Valley. It had been easier with the Italians in Youngstown whom they'd grown up knowing, knowing and liking, but the tough guys out here were a different breed. Western. Not lawbreakers like the mob, but they didn't have to be. Out here, they wrote the laws. The congressmen were their brothers-in-law.

And B. would help with them, Roy could see—the new B., with Ned by his side. B. laughed at their jokes, and Ned had lunch with their wives, and together they took them all out to dinners. Hell, said Roy one day, sitting in the new White Brothers office, trying to get some variance for a mandated parking lot, B. should ask the city councilman and his wife to tennis. Just like the Elks, said Roy, only Palm Springs–style.

"You should pick up a racket yourself," B. said to Roy, "try to get in shape."

"Are you kidding? You think I'm an overgrown kid like you, to go chasing a little ball with a little racket?"

"Hey, I thought we left the rackets back home," interceded Mel, playing the perfect third. The defuser. B. looked at Roy, but realized that he didn't care enough to get angry. Realized he felt almost sorry for him.

Loser, B. didn't say, but Roy felt it. And that night, he called Rhonda. "Who was that woman you said I should call?"

When Rhonda had first told him that she—"that woman"—had come out to spend the winter at La Quinta, Roy had forestalled any matchmaking. "She's not my type," he said.

"But you haven't met her!"

"I don't have to!" he said. But in fact he had met her or at least seen her, years ago, in Youngstown. Red-haired, with a certain glamour, married to a well-off jeweler, she lived on the same street as Ned, but unlike Ned, had had a happy marriage. The country club life, the golf—she was women's champion for a while—the travel. She and her husband had met at the University of Michigan. She was a founding member of Lit Youngstown, a local book club.

And Roy was right: she was not his type. But her husband had died suddenly, a year or so ago. She—Jo—must have been lonely enough, desperate enough, to suspend disbelief when Roy showed up with his teasing smile, and started calling her "Red." As for Roy, it was a play, a gambit, the idea being to trump B.'s Ned with his Red, and take back the reins at White Brothers, now Inc. And with her coiffed red hair and steel-blue eyes, expensive silk print blouses from Saks and Neiman's, more Palm Beach than Palm Springs, it could be argued that she left Ned, in her bright California cottons, in the dust.

But what really clinched it for Roy was the way she treated Ned and B., with a thinly veiled disdain. She laughed at their colorful condo—"Did they bring in the kindergarten to decorate?"—and Ned's puka beads and silver chains. "Next she'll be making paper flowers." And when Ned did show up one evening with some paper flowers, Roy and Jo burst out laughing, and B. and Ned stood by smiling uneasily, not quite getting the joke.

"No, nothing," said Roy, but soon after that, he asked Jo to marry him. Apparently her grown children had strongly objected, but Ned thought they seemed happy together. Jo laughing at Roy's jokes, he opening her car door, mixing her drinks—"Red and Royal," his given name, as she had started calling him.

They bought a condo near to B. and Ned's, and Jo played golf, and found a bridge game. Roy too bought some clubs and went out with her late afternoons, as the sun was turning the mountains that blue that they'd all paid for. And Ned, though surprised at the match, could see how the two of them, sharks both, could, possibly, swim through life together.

Or could have, if Roy had continued playing "Royal."

And, to be fair, if Jo had kept being "Red."

One inch of give on either side could have done it, as with so much of life. World War I. The shelling of the Parthenon. Needless, although in this case, it was, admittedly, hard to see how Jo, a committed social climber, and Roy, a downward-seeking dog, could have gone out on a second date, let alone have gotten married.

What were they thinking? But they weren't thinking, they were each of them trotting out private, almost impersonal yearnings, and hoping that they would take. Could he tame this kind of shrew and top B.? Could she shock her world *un peu* and take on this kind of player? Romantic notions both, in their way, but neither Roy nor Jo was romantic enough to go the distance. Sentimental, yes— "Royal and Red"—which works in plenty of cases. Though maybe less often with those whose origin story starts with a prenup, and is, thus, rooted in distrust.

One night toward the end, Ned and B. had agreed to meet them for dinner. Jo insisted on Le Vallauris, a pretentious new French restaurant in Palm Springs, exactly the kind of place that didn't work for the White brothers. If they were going to spend money, they expected to be well greeted, for starters, but the maître d' had already snubbed Roy as they were walking in the door. Roy had tried a little joke about the guy's stiff tux in the heat—no dice. He didn't even acknowledge the attempt. Just took a look at the open shirts and white shoes, and showed them to a table facing the kitchen.

Ned told B. afterward that her jury was still out on whether it was better to try to change tables—which rarely worked—or make the best of it. Pretend it was all right, in hopes of preserving the evening. In this case, it devolved into the worst of all outcomes. A change of table was demanded. The demand was unmet.

"Oh, come on, Roy"—not "Royal," Ned noticed—"just for once be nice," said Jo, who was the one facing out, into the dining room. When the wine guy came over, Roy and B. wanted vodka, but it turned out the place didn't have a full liquor license. Roy was ready to cut his losses right then, and they probably should have, but, "What have you got?" B. asked, and the snotty little bastard began to read, in a monotone, down the five-page wine list till Ned finally suggested some champagne.

"Californian," put in Roy.

"No such thing," rapped back the steward.

"Something sparkling," said Ned, and the steward brought them something from Napa that was barely chilled, and that the men refused to drink. Ned called for ice, and Jo got a beautifully chilled glass of Chablis and when the sole arrived, it wasn't fileted, so back it went, and by the time the dessert rolled around, the waiter didn't even bother with the menu, just the check.

"We should have gone to the Sizzler," said Jo to the maître d' as they were leaving, which Ned considered a breach of loyalty. But B. stepped in—"Call us when you get some booze," so they left with a laugh, though Ned was glad they'd brought their own car. Wouldn't have wanted to have to ride home in what was sure to be a stony silence, even in Jo's new powder-blue Mercedes.

The first one any of the White brothers had ever been in, by the way. Apparently she'd bought it with her own money.

Jo and Roy came over a few evenings later, for drinks, and Ned thought they'd patched it up. Jo looked really pretty, in one of her good silk blouses, and white pants. Well cut, the whole ensemble. Emerald earrings that picked up her eyes—her late husband the jeweler—and a clunky gold bracelet. She was clearly making an effort, laughing at Roy's jokes.

And Roy too had seemed in good spirits that night, teasing her, calling her "Red." B. poured them some of his new fancy vodka, and they drank. *"Cin cin!"* Jo had called out, gamely.

"Cin cin!" Ned answered.

"On the chin," said Roy, but without looking at Jo, which wasn't like him. He was the kind of man who didn't have to mean it to smile into a woman's eyes. But that night, he simply nodded all around, and then downed his drink. "Not bad." B. poured him another.

"Absolut," B. told him. It had just come on the American market. Before that, they'd all drunk Smirnoff and mixed it with tonic or orange juice, but this you drink straight, B. told Roy, who had no problem with that, and was, in fact, drinking it like water. They stayed so long that Ned went into the toy kitchen and pulled out some frozen Stouffer's, along with more potato chips and onion dip. "Perfect," said Jo, but Roy wanted a hot dog.

"Who doesn't?" B. joked back, but ate the spinach soufflé. Roy, however, stuck to the chips.

And that was probably the last time Ned saw them together. Roy told B. that the immediate cause of their split was that Jo had asked him who he'd save first if they were drowning—her or his mother. And then walked out the door when he told her.

But Ned doubted that version. Jo wasn't stupid, nor would she have expected, or even cared, to come first with Roy. She'd come first with her first husband. Her children. Her old friends. All she'd have expected from Roy was some fun, as well as another version of herself, when she thought she'd like to live as "Red" for a while.

Same too for Roy—"Royal." When he thought *"Cin cin"*

was charming, and that he, like B., could take on an elegant woman.

And there was a toughness there too that had drawn him. Her cold blue eyes, her dyed red hair. Illegal, or at least immoral, that red hair on a fifty-year-old woman, to give the edge he needed for him to possibly play out the kind of golden American twentieth century life that B. had managed to scrabble up for himself.

But whatever it was that B. and Ned had together, whatever kept them smiling into each other's eyes, had never really been there between Roy and Jo.

Do you talk to her at night in bed? Roy wished he was the kind of man to ask B. Because once the novelty had worn off, he and Jo didn't have a word to say to each other. B. had taken on Ned's children, which gave them at least a subject in common—but Roy and Jo had no common interests. There was nothing, he realized, that they liked to do together. He'd even had to get an extra TV, so she could put on *Dallas*, while he was watching the Browns beat Namath.

What really pulled back the curtain, though, was when she bought the Mercedes without consulting him. He, Roy, who might not know shit or care about French wine, but knew everything there was to know about cars, as well as how to get a deal.

He was almost speechless when she'd sped up in the car. She was excited, "in the ether," as the car salesmen put it. That state they can spot across the lot: when you can sell them, especially a woman, anything. Roy knew it too.

"Come for a ride!" called Jo.

He didn't budge. "How come you didn't ask me?"

She was surprised. "You don't like foreign cars," she said. Which was true—he didn't. He was a child of a steel town that was going to hell, thanks to ingrates like her buying foreign cars. "You been to Youngstown lately?" he asked her.

"No, why?" She had no clue, but neither did the rest of America, so he couldn't fairly hold that against her. Plus American cars were junk these days—who wouldn't rather have a Mercedes?

But that wasn't the point. The point, Roy might have argued if he'd cared a little more, was that the White brothers didn't buy foreign cars, which were taking down the whole industrial base of the country. But another truth lay beneath that as well, and how was Jo to know that her beautiful new powder-blue Mercedes would trigger in Roy the memory of another new car, that cream Eldorado, for which he now felt he'd thrown away the chance of his life?

Ned. A day or so later, as she drove up to the office to pick up B. in the Mustang convertible she was still driving, he found himself choking back tears. He could have had her, he was thinking.

He went home that night and realized that the life he was seeking with Jo was actually B.'s life with Ned, and that without her, the rest of it didn't work. The little condos, the bikes, the golf—for B., yeah. Life was good now for B., Roy could see.

But it was good for him too, if he could just throw over the table and rearrange some of the pieces. Business was booming. He, Roy, was leading the White Brothers farther out into the desert. From small apartments and trading empty lots, "rubble," they were now putting up "mini-malls." Someone at the bank introduced him as a "developer."

"Meet the developer Roy White," the banker in his suit

and tie had said to one of the bigwigs. Roy had come in in his red pants and golf shirt. "He's one of our bigger clients."

That was the day he went home and packed his bag. Jo could keep the condo, he told her. For anything else, she could call his lawyer. He spent a few nights in a hotel White Brothers owned in town, and then drove farther out, for a long weekend. He'd bought a house, he told his brothers, when he came back.

"In a weekend?"

"Hey, for twenty-nine thousand. Cash. Two acres."

B. whistled, more to please Roy than because he was impressed. He knew there were plenty of desert rats out there to the east, who'd be glad enough to sell their shacks and scrub acres for twenty-nine cash.

"Where?" asked B.

"Yucca Valley," Roy told him. The worst of the worst, B. knew by then. The most godforsaken place in a godforsaken corner. Bad scrub, no mountains, no water, just dust and washed-up Marlboro Men living in trailers. Barmaids with a film credit at the end of a long scroll. Flying saucer spotters. People who'd seen the little green men.

Roy's new home.

IX

Y ucca V alley is only twenty-seven miles from Palm Springs—not far on paper, but far enough for Roy to "slip his tether," as Jo put it to Ned. He went out there still thinking of himself as a hotshot developer. In fact, as his obituary would eventually claim, *"his passing coincided fittingly with Yucca Valley's own transition from a rural community to the center of prosperous growth White always said it would be."*

But that was both the future and debatable, and when B. and Mel drove out one day to make a reconnaissance, they felt it was a long twenty-seven miles indeed. The feeling that day was one of traveling through time as well as space, back to the thirties, to the Depression—not the one they'd known back in Ohio, but someone else's. Those poor Dust Bowl farmers they'd seen in old pictures, with broken-down windmills in the background, and hungry wives and scrawny kids. Yucca Valley looked to them more a place for rattlesnakes and jackrabbits than for strip malls. The car thermometer gave the outside reading of 110 degrees, and that was in the shade. The two White brothers in their air-conditioned Lincoln found themselves reluctant to get out of the car.

But they gamely walked the perimeter of more classic rubble that Roy wanted them to buy. Tried to see if what Roy saw in the place was what their father had seen in Palm Springs in the late sixties. True, it was a wide-open field, without much in the way of competition. No gated communities eating into this desert yet, no emerald golf courses guzzling what was left of the Colorado River in this neck of the woods. On the contrary; and Roy assured them too that whatever regulations they had out here were made to be broken.

"Like promises." He smiled at the woman on his arm. Marylou, not Jo—the opposite of Jo. A nice, quiet, bleached-out blonde who might not have finished high school. Older too than what might have been expected, given the number of trim divorcées in their fifties, even forties, who'd pitched up out there. Roy told B. he'd tried a few of those, but got tired of the Diet Coke cans cramming his refrigerator and little orange pill bottles filling up his trash. Purple and green yoga mats curling behind his sofa.

There seemed to be no danger of any of that with Marylou. She'd been "in pictures," she told B., "but nothin' you'da heard of," which he figured meant porn. He wondered briefly what her downward trajectory had entailed, from some Okie farm with the kind of American clear good looks you could still see traced through her wrinkles, looks that would have set her off along the well-worn path away from any chance of small-town happiness, straight into the ever-gaping Hollywood maw.

B. imagined it would have been the usual story with this one—from the casting couch with hopes still plausible, through maybe even a negligible role or two, leading, despite the promises, nowhere. Then some porn shoots in the Valley, which at least would have paid off some of the bills, and then who knew which path to survival she'd taken after that— escort service? Checkout girl in the supermarket?—bouncing her ever further from the center of desire, till she finally rolled to a stop here. By the time Roy came into the picture, she was cocktail-waitressing out near the Marine base, where they couldn't get anyone younger who could pass the drug test.

Roy must have come out of the blue for her, like the guardian angel she'd half given up expecting, but wasn't surprised to find out in the same kind of desert where Jesus himself had sought the light, as her pastor over at the Assembly kept reminding them. B. noticed she clung to Roy's arm like it was a life raft, and he figured she too answered for Roy at this point.

The kind of nice, uncomplicated woman who was glad enough for the place to lay her head, rent-free, no further questions asked. Roy barely took notice of her that day, as he walked his brothers around the empty "parcel," as he was already calling it.

And maybe he was right about that, B. decided, as he stood in the middle with narrowed eyes, looking out beyond. No one would call this the promised land, but once you got to the untouched parts, high chaparral desert, there was that harmony and symmetry that pertain to all land in its natural state. There were the Joshua trees, weird to untutored eyes, and the Mojave yuccas that Ned's daughter told him were called "Spanish bayonets." If you touched them, they'd prick the hell out of your finger, but when they bloomed in the spring, the tall stocks of white flowers were delicate and perfumed the air around them.

Though here, on Roy's "parcel," they'd already been half-cut and left to look plain ugly. Tough and sharp and hacked away—"I already talked to the mayor," Roy was saying. "They're going to hold their Grubstake Days out here, and rent it from us till we put something up."

If we buy it, thought B., but he knew they'd buy it. That's what White Brothers did. Bought the junk, the trash.

"What the hell are Grubstake Days?" asked Mel, but just to talk, since he had to know—one of those fake-o cutesy western-style swarm-ups, with a shooting gallery, cotton candy, maybe a hometown rodeo. Everyone walking around in the cowboy boots they'd picked up on markdown over at the Boot Barn.

"Did he sign something?" B. asked. "The mayor?"

"*She*," said Roy with his smile—high Roy, the essential Roy, thought B. He looked like the cat who'd swallowed the canary. He told his brothers that Yucca Valley was his kind of place.

"So you're a hick at heart? A cowboy?" Mel had joked to him, but Roy just smiled at Marylou and said, "What do you think?"

And she smiled back and said, "He's gettin' real good at the two-step over at Pappy and Harriet's," and B. and Mel got back into the Lincoln and drove west so fast they got a ticket. It was worth it, though, and they agreed to split it. White Brothers, anyway, would pay.

A few months later, B. got an urgent call from his lawyer to turn on the nightly news. Roy had cut down some protected Joshua trees, and someone had called the cops on him.

He was nearly thrown into jail, should have been. It

was a federal—or at least a state—crime. But the town had turned out for him in force. The local news too, with TV cameras rolling.

B. and Ned watched in astonishment—Roy outside the local courthouse, talking to a reporter, saying, "Hell, they looked like weeds to me." A crowd of ragtag desert rats pushing up behind him—"You tell 'em, Roy!" "Buncha weeds," and so on. Roy playing what must have been his dream role: a tough-talking John Wayne, but with money instead of a gun in his pocket and the town behind him. Even the mayor came tripping out in her high heels for the cameras: "Hey, you all talk about politicians being in bed with people. Well, I would love to be in bed with Roy White!"

"She is," said B., but Ned thought not. She was a little too sharp for Roy these days, a little too young. No way he could handle that mayor in bed.

"So now it's just 'illegal and fattening,'" said B. White Brothers wrote the check to the BLM for the fine that Roy had incurred. Fast enough so they didn't haul him into San Bernardino, where his little tough-guy act might not play the way it had in Yucca Valley.

Still, in Yucca Valley, Roy seemed to have it all figured out. He was now living in a sprawling white mansion atop the only hill in town. The guy who'd bought the land—from Roy —and then built the house had "gone bust," as Roy put it, and he'd seen it coming. Had even loaned him the cash for the kind of marble he, Roy, wanted in his bathrooms. The guy tried to sell it back to him, but Roy had waited and then scooped it up at auction. He was Romanian or Bulgarian, apparently, though everyone called him Russian.

Russian Mafia, B. had heard, but when he mentioned changing the locks, Roy just laughed. He was still making money for White Brothers in Yucca Valley, but where you could find him most days now was sitting on an old leather chair with the stuffing coming out, in front of a dusty store-front in downtown Yucca, under a broken sign that said ANTIQUES. A place that he'd bought for White Brothers to rent out.

But as he'd walked through the clutter, the chipped china and tattered old quilts, special-issue whiskey bottles, big band record albums still in their plush white cases, and sculpture upon sculpture of bucking broncos, some red, some brass, all fake, made—had to be—for Texas chicken farmers who'd hit oil out in the backyard, as he walked through this place, something had sounded, some distant chime that all along he knew he'd hear out here eventually—why he'd come here. An echo of something he couldn't quite name. His father. Life when he was young. Home.

So instead of clearing out that junk and renting to a Lamps Plus, he propped an old leather chair in the door-way and settled himself in. Cigar in his mouth, roll of bills in his pocket, waiting for the "rabbits," as he called them, to pull up with something to sell.

Roy paid low, but he paid cash, which few of his fel-low Yucca Valleyites could resist. They'd roll in, in their decrepit "vintage" BMWs and their dusty pickups with whatever they could scrounge up that might turn to cash. When B. was there one day, a woman came in with her grandmother's moonstone brooch, and a man with the last of the "Remingtons" he'd probably stolen, Roy told B., off a truck near Desert Hot Springs. When he protested the price, Roy took him into the back and showed him the three others he'd already bought that week, and then the guy had just shrugged the way they all did, and held out his hand.

"Not bad," said B., looking at the Remington. A cowboy on a bronco.

"Fake," said Roy, but B. took it anyway, along with the moonstone pin for Ned, who gave it to a niece who liked Victorian jewelry. He asked Roy how the business was doing out there, meaning White Brothers.

But Roy had just laughed and said, as if B. were a stranger asking about his junk shop, "Hey, it keeps me going." He told B. how a couple of days ago a guy he'd brought out from Ohio to do odd jobs for him, someone from their Cleveland Auto Wrecking days, had had his tools stolen out of his truck his first night in town.

The poor guy was desperate. "My life," he'd said to Roy, who didn't have to be told what an independent working-man's tools meant to him.

Roy told him to pull up a chair out front with him and wait. And sure enough, around midmorning, some kids pulled up in a pickup and asked if they wanted to buy some tools.

Roy turned to his guy. "Go get 'em."

"Just like that?" he said.

"Sure"—Roy nodded—"if they're yours," but he knew they were. No one out there sold his tools. Roy thanked the kids for returning stolen goods, gave them a fiver, and they peeled off.

"Roy White." People out there shook their heads.

"He sits there in that broken-down chair like a prince with a stick," Mel said to B., when he came back from a visit. "Fatter 'n hell, too."

"Fat and happy," said B. to Ned. It seemed so improbable, so unlikely—how Roy had found his way back to junk in the worst corner of the desert, where he'd reinvented himself as leading citizen, which, given the cast of characters out there, he was. So much so, that one day White Brothers got a call. Roy had apparently been kidnapped. The police were searching.

By the time B. and Ned got out there, a patrolman had already found him, locked in the trunk of his Lincoln, out on a dead-end track in the desert. The sun was blazing, and Roy was in his eighties and overweight. They'd radioed for an ambulance, but after some water and a little time in the air-conditioned police car, Roy insisted he was fine. As B. was driving him home in the Lincoln, a smile crept across his face.

He pulled a fifty-thousand-dollar cashier's check from his shirt pocket. The fact that the kidnappers had grabbed a couple of hundred dollars' cash from his pants pocket but missed the check was what had kept him going in that trunk, he said. "Laughing my ass off," he told B.

Everyone figured it was the "Russians"—there were two of them who'd come to his house, masked, Marylou had told the police, speaking a foreign language. When B. called a few days later to ask if they'd been caught, Roy just laughed and said there was nothing to worry about, they were "long gone," leaving B. to wonder what part of the story Roy hadn't told him. And when it happened again—incredibly, but true—the same policeman drove out to the same road in the desert, found Roy's car, and called out to the trunk, half joking, "Roy White, are you in there?"

And that's how Roy played it, more as a joke than anything else. Ned said she was going to install a minibar in

Roy's trunk, but Mel and B. tried to convince him—unsuc-cessfully—to get security. He said some of his pals were looking out for him now, and he was "just fine." Though what he meant by "fine" B. started to wonder, after he got a call from the bank—a White Brothers account out of Yucca Valley that was supposed to have several hundred thousand dollars was overdrawn.

B. called a forensic accountant and drove out to Roy's office. He found a gleaming Ducati parked outside, and Roy's so-called office manager in hot pink spandex on an exercise bike in the corner. A guy they'd never seen before was laughing into Roy's phone, his feet on Roy's desk. He and the office manager exchanged looks when B. asked for the books.

It turned out to be a straightforward swindle, "amateur hour," according to the forensic accountant. While Roy was playing Sam White down at his junk shop on Main Street, extracting nickels and dimes from the local desperadoes, all these rookies back in his office had to do was wait for the rent checks to roll in in the U.S. mail, slit the enve-lopes, forge Roy's signature, and then deposit the money into their own account rather than White Brothers'. It had been going on for a couple of years.

"What the hell were you thinking?" B. couldn't stop himself from asking Roy, as they faced the bookkeeper and her young boyfriend in court. Their sole possession worth anything was the Ducati, which ended up occupying space in one of B.'s garages for a while, as part of the reparations. The bookkeeper was also required to pay back fifty dol-lars a month, eked from her ex-husband's pension that she wouldn't be needing anyway in prison.

But Roy didn't answer—what was there to say? That he

was too busy to look over his own books? That real estate investments were nothing to him, once he'd drifted back to junk?

Mel asked B. what he thought Sam White would have said about that—both the junk store and the embezzlement. B. just shook his head. They were old men now, over eighty, all of them, but their father's wrath still loomed.

That a son of his would have let things go like that, for so long and for so much, like a rich boy born with a silver spoon in his mouth—the kind of spoon Sam White had had to scrape for, through muck and junk heaps, for half his life. What he'd crossed the sea without, alone at thirteen, what he'd lost his house for want thereof, been put into the street over, he and his family. And though in the end it had worked out for him—Sam White had died in a million-dollar house in Beverly Hills—he'd never once taken his eyes off the books. Never lost count of all those barley bundles.

Roy died soon after that, "*a local legend*," according to the *Hi-Desert Star*. B. was quoted saying that "*Roy liked to do things his own way*," and the piece went on to say that "*many folks here who tried to persuade White otherwise still speak of him as an obstinate opponent*." But Ned, who'd known another side of Roy, did him one last favor by adding her own quote: "*People who knew him liked him, and Roy really loved Yucca Valley, and the people in it*."

The funeral took place in Los Angeles. Sam White had bought them all "condominiums," as they joked, using a word they'd first learned in California, at the Forest Lawn Cemetery, in the "columbarium," a word Ned hoped she'd never learn. The family gathered, and they slid Roy's ashes into the compartment next to his mother. B. told Ned he was glad enough that they'd done it there. Glad not to have to trek back out to Yucca Valley in the heat, already in April.

They usually took the coast road home, but since they were already in the Valley, they decided to stick with the 101 up to Santa Barbara. There'd been no one to host a gathering afterward—Rhonda had died of emphysema a few years back—so they agreed to stop with Mel and his new wife at the Sportsmen's Lodge on Ventura Boulevard in Studio City, where Sam White had hosted a wedding brunch for B. and Ned all those years ago.

It had seemed so glamorous to her at the time, exotic with a little lake behind the place, where John Wayne, Tallulah Bankhead, and Bette Davis used to bait hooks with liverwurst and sip martinis as they fished for dinner, and Studio City too had glamorous connotations in those days. Now the glitter and the lake were both gone, and the food had turned generic. Not that they minded, really—B. and Mel were glad enough for steaks and fries and their vodkas, "doubles, rocks on the side, bucket glasses"—too many, in fact. Ned had to drive home.

B. fell asleep as they were inching through Thousand Oaks, the part where the drought-blighted eucalyptus trees for some reason reminded Ned of home. Ohio, autumn, and it was then, alone in spirit if not in body, that she allowed herself to think freely about Roy for the first time in many years. They'd put his ashes in that drawer at the cemetery that day, but he'd been in a drawer for her since he'd left for California, in 1963.

And now, as she cautiously pulled it open and took a look inside, a real look rather than one necessarily blinkered by her marriage to his brother, she found nothing but ashes there as well—nothing to harm, or even interest, her anymore. She was surprised, a little, but realized that it was probably the fact that the subject had always been untouchable, under such an absolute taboo, between her and B. that had kept her thinking maybe there was still something alive. A spark, an ember.

Long after there was nothing, nothing, left between her and Roy. For his part, he didn't seem to like the woman she had become with B.—a woman laughing, a woman having fun. It came to her that Roy didn't like happy women. Thank God she hadn't had to learn that the hard way.

Nor did she have any further appetite for cruel, selfish men, no matter how they smiled, how light their touch on her arm. She saw that she could have opened that drawer years ago. Not that it mattered much—it wasn't as if she and Roy would have achieved some level of friendship. Or even found anything to talk about.

But she had to admit she admired the way Roy had worked his life out, in the end. It was almost Zen, she was thinking as she hit the long, slow descent into Camarillo. Ten years ago there was no one here, but now the road was crowded. Bumper-to-bumper going through what didn't even used to be a town.

Zen, the way Roy had let much of what the rest of them had worked for all their lives just sort of fall away. Family ties—his brothers, his daughter. He barely knew her children.

And the money, the fact that he'd been swindled, that he hadn't been watching his books—wasn't that Zen too, in a way? What Sam White's sons had been schooled to do was watch their money. Hadn't Roy simply moved on from all that?

And hadn't he, in the end, followed his bliss? He loved his junk shop, his "antiques." As the paper put it, " . . . *the newer arrivals to Yucca Valley may not recognize White's name, but many might have furnished their houses with items from either one of his two used furniture and appliance stores, one in Yucca Valley and one in Twentynine Palms.*"

"What appliance store?" Mel had said to B., over lunch, as they read the obituary. B. just shook his head—one more of Roy's little swindles. He must have opened it in one of the White Brothers' properties he'd claimed they couldn't rent in Twentynine Palms. Who knew?

But who cared? They'd sell it now, sell everything that was left in that down-market corner of the desert that Roy had found to call home, and move on—White Brothers too. Mel was going blind. B. was driving down only every other week or so. Sometimes less. He wouldn't miss Yucca Valley, he told Ned, which she figured meant Roy too.

The sun was going down as they continued up the 101, through the town of Santa Barbara. The freeway cut like a gash through the heart of the small city, separating beach from mountains, not to mention the noise from the relentless traffic, the fumes. Ned's daughter said she dreamed of the day when the Greens would shut the road down, but B. told her not to hold her breath. The same people who'd pushed it through once would push it through again. Developers. Lobbyists. The ones who always got their way.

As they exited the highway and turned toward the beach and their White House, B. woke up and Ned whispered a goodbye to Roy. "Rest in peace," she breathed, a peace Roy seemed to have found at last.

*   *   *

Though a few weeks later, they got a call from Marylou. "Can you come out?" she asked.

B. figured she was a woman who didn't make requests without a reason, and said he could.

"That's good, because I want you to see some stuff we found in the wall beside Roy's bed."

"What kind of stuff?"

"Silver. Coins, bars—"

"In the wall?" He believed her, though. It was pure Roy. His version of taking it with him.

"Yeah, we found it—"

"Who's 'we'?" asked B., going for the car keys.

"Me and my son," said Marylou.

B. drove the three and a half hours down to Roy's house on the hill in Yucca Valley that day. Marylou was in some kind of old wrapper and didn't seem to have combed her hair. She missed Roy, she told him.

When they got to the bedroom, the crummy drywall had been partially torn out. She'd got her son to do it, she said, since Roy had said something about it just before he died, and she'd got to thinking.

Was that true? B. wondered. Or was there something else going on here? There was what looked like a horde of silver behind the wall. B. wondered who Roy had found to stow it there for him. Someone who'd kidnapped him, twice? Or someone he could trust not to hit him over the head and throw him into the trunk of his car? Maybe that was the subtext of the story about the guy and his tools, bringing him out here from Ohio in the first place. Roy laughing up his sleeve at his brothers, one more time.

"What'd he say?" B. asked Marylou.

"Something about silver. Though in the end, it was kinda hard to hear him. He was saying to call you."

And why she did call was an enduring mystery to B. and Ned. Why she didn't just get her son to bring over his truck in the dead of night and clean the place out, they never understood. B. thought she'd probably skimmed some off the top, which would have been good, said Ned, because when Roy's will was read, Marylou wasn't even mentioned. It was as if he'd forgotten that she'd existed, at least as part of his life.

Ned insisted that she be given a White Brothers pension. Silver or no silver, she'd earned it, Ned said.

B. agreed. "Roy got lucky," he said. A nice woman to wash his face and close his eyes at the end.

But Zen? Ned was privately embarrassed by her sappy construct. A few nights later, they were having supper at the country club near their house in Santa Barbara. The waiter brought B. his vodka, just the way he liked it, Grey Goose these days. Ned asked for tequila, but in a stem glass. The waiter knew, he smiled, with a few olives on the side.

Ned mentioned the silver again—"What do you make of it?"—but B. just shrugged, and then some friends came over and joined them. And B. was done talking about Roy.

Though Ned would have liked another word or two. Would have liked to hear him saying, "Zen, my ass," and laughing.

Ned lifted her glass. She was going to say, *Namaste, Roy*, as a joke, but glanced at B. and changed her mind.

"To us," she said.

o fim